WHAT IF THE MAFIA AND FBI JOINED FORCES TO ASSASSINATE HITLER IN 1938? COULD IT HAVE SUCCEEDED? COULD IT HAVE PREVENTED WWII? COULD IT HAVE CHANGED THE WORLD?

The FBI colludes with the mafia to assassinate Hitler in the spring of 1938 during a state visit to Italy. Bugsy Siegel and his accomplice, a secret agent to keep the gangster's volatile nature from erupting, are chosen to carry out the deed. With the help of the Italian mafia, conned into thinking the target is their bitter enemy Mussolini, the pair must avoid rival gangs and a wily Italian police inspector to avoid being caught or killed before they can even get close to Hitler. No one could have predicted the calamitous events their mission unleashes.

"...nations that play chess with world leaders should beware; toppling the King may just be the beginning...The author's personal insight makes *Payback* a great novel of what might have been." —*Ian Hall, author of the Avenging Steel series.*

"*Payback* is a fascinating alternative history which turns what we know of World War II on its head. Gangsters and Hitler - what could go wrong? Read Payback to find out!"—*James R Benn, author Rag and Bone.*

"...Real historical figures blend seamlessly with fictional ones, and everyone is believable...In the long tradition of Axis victories in the Alt-History genre, Italy is often overlooked. Michael FitzGerald changes that with *Payback,* a novel filled with strong characters, excellent research and surprising twists and turns."—*Sandra Saidak, author of From the Ashes.*

"...Bugsy Siegel, a hitman for the American Mafia, and Luigi Carmona, a far less psychotic but no less competent killer, travel to Mussolini's Rome before the outbreak of World War II on a mission of assassination...a page-turner of a thriller [and]an alternate history novel that asks us whether great men control history or...are controlled by it..." —*David Dvorkin, Author of Budspy.*

"*Payback* is a first-rate thriller. Michael FitzGerald's tale of World War II intrigue and daring keeps the heart racing to the very last page."—*James Thayer, author S-Day.*

"...a great read with an amazing plot that kept me always wanting more. It's a great story about Hitler, Mussolini, gangsters and an FBI agent that held my interest till the end..."—*David Avoura King - Author Hitler Out of Time.*

"...one of the most original 'what if' novels since *Fatherland*...explores the unique possibility that if Adolf Hitler were assassinated before his grip on Germany tightened then there would be a power vacuum in Europe of immense proportions. His addition of American mafia figures brings a colorful new level to this intriguing novel."—*Kim Kinrade, Author Rockets of the Reich.*

PAYBACK

Michael FitzGerald

Moonshine Cove Publishing, LLC
Abbeville, South Carolina U.S.A.

This book is a work of fiction. Names, characters, places and incidents are products of the author's imagination or are used fictitiously. Any resemblance to actual events, locales or persons, living or dead, is entirely coincidental.

ISBN: 978-1-945181-00-9
Library of Congress Control Number: 2016916471
Copyright 2016 by Michael FitzGerald

Book cover and interior design by Moonshine Cove staff, cover image public domain.

Other Works

The Nazi Occult War

Storm Troopers of Satan

Alien Arrival

Ragged London

Adolf Hitler, A Portrait

The Making of Modern Streatham

American Destiny, From Adam to Obama

ABOUT THE AUTHOR

Michael FitzGerald has appeared on television and radio programs about WWII. He has an honours degree in philosophy and is an authority on the Third Reich. He has been a delegate at the Cambridge History Festival. Michael FitzGerald has also provided research for television programs, written articles for Wikipedia and been an expert at Allexperts.com.

https://www.facebook.com/mikefitzauthor?fref=nf

https://twitter.com/mikefitzauthor

https://www.pinterest.com/fitzgerald2851/

mikefitzuk.wordpress.com/

http://mikefitzauthor.blogspot.com

Payback

1

Killing came easy to Frank Costello but even he was shocked when he heard the target. On a day in March 1938 when the sky drizzled he made his way towards a bench in Central Park. His two bodyguards held an umbrella over him to shield him from the rain.

He was on time — 14.00 hours

He paused within sight of the bench and stared intently at the man wearing a raincoat sitting there patiently at the pre-planned meeting point.

"Mr Costello," the seated man said, rising to greet him. "Special Agent Jones."

Costello refused the offer of a handshake. He sat down on the bench and glared at his unwanted companion.

"Well, Mr. FBI man, what do you want with me?"

Jones looked at the two bodyguards who stood behind the bench.

"You won't need them," he said. "I'm not here on police business."

Costello lit a cigar and puffed away.

"Of course you are. You're a cop. Police business is all you know. And you Feds are the worst of the lot. You're obviously trying to set me up for something. Well, you're wasting your time. You can go to hell!"

Jones stood up.

"Frisk me if you want. I'm not wearing a wire and I'm not trying to trick you. I want to put a proposition to you."

"What sort of proposition?"

"It's a matter of national importance. We need to talk alone. Ask your men to step away."

Costello turned to his two henchmen.

"Take a walk. But not too far."

Once they were out of earshot Jones lit up a cigarette.

"Mr Costello, we want your organization to kill someone for us."

Costello stared at him for a moment and then burst out laughing.

"Is this a joke? I thought you guys got paid to stop murder, not commission it."

"You read the papers, don't you? Well..."

Costello's face flushed with anger and the veins on his forehead stood out. He balled his hand into a fist and for a moment seemed about to strike Jones. Instead he yelled at the FBI man.

"You trying to make out I'm dumb or something?"

"Hear me out," Jones said. "You didn't let me finish. Europe is on the brink of war and the U.S. will be dragged into it."

"What's that got to do with me?"

Costello stood up and prepared to leave.

"Please sit down and let me explain. If there's another war a lot of people are going to die. But if we kill just one man there won't be any war."

"You think killing one man will stop a war? Anyway it's none of my damn business. Do your own dirty work! What's in it for me, anyway?"

"We'd make it worth your while. The police would ease off on your people and you'd be handsomely rewarded for your assistance."

The cops have been trying to bust my rackets lately, Costello thought. And who doesn't want more money? What's his angle, though?

"Who is it you want killed, anyway?"

"The target is Hitler and we want you to help us kill him."

Costello stared at him and the cigar fell from his hand and landed on the ground. When he recovered from the shock he asked him the obvious question.

"Why don't you kill him yourself?"

"We don't want it to look like a political killing."

"Why not? That's exactly what it is."

The agent began to sweat in spite of the cold as he sensed that Costello was still unhappy about the idea.

"If the world knows the United States organized the assassination of Hitler it would mean big problems for us. We might end up at war with Germany. The public would not support our actions."

"Not my problem. Anyway, it's too dangerous. You'd never get close enough to get a shot in."

"It would be dangerous but it would be worth it. You and I both know that there are Jews in your organization who'd be delighted to see him dead. People would certainly believe they might kill him."

The agent hoped he would be easier to persuade. He tried to appeal to his patriotism.

"Hitler's death has to look like a gangster killing. Let's make a deal that will benefit both of us. If you won't do it for your country do it for your Jewish friends."

Costello began to think it might be worthwhile after all.

"You'd need someone who's good with a rifle. My guys are more used to handguns."

Jones clutched at the sudden opportunity.

"We'd train him. He'd go on an intensive course with our agent and the two of them would go on the mission together. He mustn't know his partner works for the government. Let him think they're both hitmen for your organization. He'll be working with a pro so even if he misses it won't matter. Our guy will kill Hitler and he'll just be a smokescreen."

Am I doing the right thing? Will the Feds protect any shooter I give them?

"If I let you have one of my people I'd want you to guarantee his safety."

"There's never any guarantee in this line of work, Mr Costello. But his partner will be a fully trained and experienced agent and we'll have people on the ground watching out for them both and doing everything we can to bring them back safe."

"Where and when?"

"Not yet decided. We'll arrange a meeting with our agent."

"I'll think about it. Give me a few days and I'll get back to you."

Costello made a sign and his bodyguards joined him.

"Let's go," he said.

But a slight smile passed over his face for the first time. *Yes, I think I know someone crazy enough to do it.* As he walked away he wondered — could the man he had in mind carry out the plan or had he made the biggest mistake of his life?

2

As night fell and the neon sign at Pete's Bar flashed on and off two smartly dressed men sat at a table in the corner. They sat away from the main clientele to avoid being overheard.

One of the men in the bar stood at nearly six feet tall. He was handsome, immaculately dressed, and only the steel that shone behind his blue eyes gave a hint of the type of man he really was.

The other man was much shorter, standing at only five feet four, and far less physically striking than his friend. Only his cold smile revealed a will and a degree of hatred every bit as intense as that of his friend.

It was not pleasure that brought them there that evening. As they drank their third bourbon and lit up a cigarette they sat at their table quietly. They gazed out of the window and waited for the moment to strike at their enemies.

The proprietor stepped forward to serve them.

"Another drink, Mr Lansky, Mr Siegel. Or perhaps some food — on the house of course."

Lansky waved him away but without irritation.

"Another time, Pete. We've got some unfinished business ahead of us."

The two men turned away as soon as Pete had gone and gazed out of the window. Across the road stood a large brick building with its lights blazing and the door wide open to admit the long queue of people waiting outside and slowly entering.

"Look at those Nazi Germans," said Siegel. "They don't know what's going to hit them tonight!"

Lansky looked across the street and saw the queue slowly beginning to dwindle.

"Not long now."

Siegel looked at him and then glared at the crowd making its way inside the building.

"To think the Rabbi offered you money to do this, Meyer!" He laughed. "Still, I bet he was surprised when you turned him down."

"I'm sure he was. But you and I can both remember when we were kids. Just a couple of hoodlums on the street. Hell, religion never bothered either of us back then. But when the Nazis came out with all that anti-Semitic crap and I saw what they were doing to our people I felt I just had to do something about it. Crazy, isn't it? It took Hitler to make me realize I was a Jew."

He looked at the street again and then back to his friend.

"You know, this is the fourth time we've done this. But tonight is going to be the big one. There's a large crowd and it won't be easy breaking their meeting up."

"What the hell, we got plenty of muscle. I reckon I can take on at least twenty of those guys just on my own!"

"Maybe."

He gazed out of the window and saw that the last person in the queue had finally entered the building.

"Come on, let's go."

"Yeah, it's showtime!"

The two men left the bar and made their way into the darkness of the street. They were about to go into battle and a sense of mounting excitement filled them both.

3

The wind whipped across from the Hudson River and the air had the oppressive feel of weather before an impending thunderstorm. The men who stood outside the assembly hall radiated the same sense of charged electrical tension. The cold air bit into their bones, its chill mingling with the inner ice of fear as they contemplated what lay ahead. In a few minutes the men would enter the hall and face their enemies directly. Full of a mixture of courage and belief in the rightness of their cause, they longed for the sharp release of action to free them from the frozen immobility in which they lingered, the men as sharp and eager as arrows desiring their imminent departure from the poised tension of the bow.

The fifteen Jews who were about to gatecrash the meeting of the pro-Nazi German American Bund were not "respectable" citizens. All of them, especially the two leaders of the evening's mayhem, were well known to the police and the FBI. Not one of them earned his living honestly. They ran gambling, protection rackets, prostitution and loan sharking. Not one of them would have thought twice about killing another person and many of the fifteen present already had a number of unsolved homicides against their name.

Benjamin Siegel, like the rest of the men who planning to break up the Nazi meeting, was a professional criminal, a gangster. At only thirty-two years old he was one of the most senior members of the American Mafia, like his friend Meyer Lansky.

Siegel was a hitman, a bruiser, an enforcer. He would do anything and not even give it a thought.

The people inside the hall were eagerly awaiting the speaker's address and had no idea that anything out of the ordinary was about to happen. There were unaware that only a short distance away fifteen young Jews were lurking, determined to prevent the meeting from taking place

In the sky above a rumble of thunder broke out and a flash of lightning stabbed the night sky. As if this was some kind of sign for action, Lansky turned to his friend.

"Let's do it."

The ground floor of the building was a large hall with chairs where the audience of three hundred sat listening to a speaker holding forth. On the stage a swastika hung above his head and a large picture of Hitler was prominently displayed.

As the young Jews entered the crowd turned round and stared at the unexpected visitors. Lansky pointed to the ground floor windows and the men began opening them.

"We're taking back our country," shouted Siegel, "If you like Germany so much why don't you go back there?"

He then turned to the audience and fixed them with a fierce stare from his penetrating blue eyes.

"Get your women out of here! Fighting's a man's job!"

The women began to scream as they heard his words and realized there was going to be a brawl. Reluctantly they stood up and began moving towards the exit. Some of them were sobbing hysterically and trying to drag their husbands away with them before the trouble started in earnest.

The intruders began throwing people out of the open ground floor windows. The attackers might have been completely outnumbered but their bravery, the sheer surprise of their appearance and the violence of their attack upon the meeting more than made up for it. Fists flew and arms grabbed members of the audience, sending them crashing on to the street.

There were a number of Brownshirts near the front of the hall and they moved quickly to try and quell the invasion. The attackers began by using their fists but with the approach of the Nazi bodyguards they picked up chairs and used them as weapons. They drove them into the men's stomachs, smashed them over their head and employed them as makeshift clubs.

The Brownshirts waded into the attackers, grabbing chairs in their turn. The meeting was descending into a chaotic brawl and the Nazis were every bit as aggressive as the intruders. In spite of their small numbers the fifteen Jews created mayhem out of all proportion to the size of their group.

Benny Siegel, utterly fearless, carved his way through the crowd with brutal, demented violence. Intent upon bringing the confrontation to an abrupt climax, he broke away and marched straight ahead. He gazed right into the nervous eyes of the speaker who summoned his bodyguards to protect him as the Jew advanced upon the stage.

Siegel strode right up to the swastika banner and hurled it on the ground. None of the Nazis stopped him, instead gazing in stunned disbelief. How could one man cause so much destruction in his wake? Then he seized a picture of Hitler and trampled it under his feet.

The speaker and his six henchmen looked at him and hesitated. There were seven of them and he was just one man. In spite of the odds they knew he was capable of causing enough violence to incapacitate most if not all of them..

The speaker turned away and spoke to the Brownshirts and his followers generally.

"Everyone out!" he shouted.

No one moved towards Siegel as he stood there punching the air in triumph. Flanked by his bodyguards the speaker left rapidly. The rest of the audience abandoned the fight, moving towards the exit in search of sanctuary, now intent only on returning to their homes before they needed the attention of the local hospitals.

As the last stragglers made their way out of the meeting, Siegel hurled a final insult at them.

"Some Master Race you turned out to be!"

The fifteen Jews made their way out of the hall just minutes before the first police cars reached the now abandoned building.

"Great job, guys!" said Lansky.

Then the group parted to go its separate ways. Lansky and Siegel walked together for a while.

A frown passed over Siegel's face.

"You know, we could put a stop to all this right now if we just sent over a guy to Germany and whacked Hitler. That'd end it for sure!"

Lansky looked at his friend with a resigned expression on his face.

"Not this again. Enough already! We talked about this before. It's too dangerous."

"I'd die happy knowing I'd knocked off that son of a bitch!"

"You think I don't want him dead every bit as much as you do? Our job is to keep the Nazis out of America. Now let's get out of here before the cops catch us!"

The two men parted with a feeling of triumph after the night's events. Breaking up a meeting of Nazis in New York might be only a small thing in itself but to Lansky and Siegel it was their contribution to a crusade against Hitler and his regime. They might not be able to harm him directly but at least they could attack his supporters in America.

After Siegel had said goodbye to his friend he made his way to the luxury suite he maintained in one of New York City's classiest hotels. He entered it in high spirits, the adrenalin rush he felt after the night's events putting him into almost a state of ecstasy. Standing beside the tub he hesitated briefly over which oil to use. Then he laid in the bath and soaked away his cuts and bruises in the warm water.

4

Morning came upon New York at last but Siegel still slept, if hardly the sleep of the just, at least with the quiet satisfaction of a man who has done his job well. Dressing with his usual fussiness, taking an eternity to comb his hair exactly the way he wanted, he emerged at lunchtime wearing his hound's tooth check suit and a typically gaudy tie. Face cream was lovingly applied to improve his already film star looks. At last after endless preparation he was ready to face the world.

The slickly groomed hair, hand-made suit and shoes and the immaculate way in which everything fitted him perfectly made him look like a dandy. His sparkling eyes and ready smile gave the impression of an easy-going and happy-go-lucky type of man.

Wandering out of the hotel he hailed a cab to an uptown restaurant. He knew it was a favourite eating place of his two best friends. He was almost at the door of the restaurant when a man bumped into him in the street accidentally. The transformation was immediate and terrifying.

"Why don't you look where you're going, asshole?"

The cold glare on Siegel's face froze the man into a stunned silence and immobility. For a moment he thought he was about to be physically attacked.

"I'm sorry," he said in a trembling voice.

"Piss off!"

He pushed the man out of the way before composing himself as he turned towards the door. When he entered the restaurant the owner recognized him immediately.

"Mr Siegel," he said, almost bowing. "Always a pleasure to have you here."

Siegel smiled at him, once more the affable and relaxed man he had been only a few minutes before. His anger had gone as quickly as it had appeared.

"Hi, Tony."

The proprietor summoned a member of staff to take his hat and coat and then escorted him personally to his table. Lansky and Costello were already sitting there and talking animatedly over a glass of red wine.

"Good to see you, Benny," said Costello. "Had a good night?"

Siegel grinned.

"The best! But I guess Meyer told you about that already!"

"He mentioned something about it, yeah."

Costello snapped his fingers and the waiter almost ran to the table.

"Another bottle of red wine. What are you eating today?"

"I'll take the steak and a small salad."

The waiter disappeared with the order and the three men chatted amiably. The restaurant proprietor hovered beside the table and whispered some news.

"I just heard on the radio that Hitler has marched into Austria without any opposition. Thousands of people are fleeing the country or under arrest. Especially..." he hesitated for a moment, "Jewish people."

Siegel banged his glass of wine on the table with such force and fury that it shattered. He leapt up from his chair and picked up the steak knife from his plate before stabbing the meat with it.

"That bastard Hitler!" he yelled.

He was shaking with rage and the eyes in his head stared with the cold fire of a professional killer in search of revenge. Lansky and Costello gazed at each other as they recognized the signs that he was on the point of losing all control.

Siegel sat down at the table and toyed with the remains of his steak. He had lost his appetite now that Hitler was spreading his hateful Nazi empire further afield. He lit a cigarette and blew smoke rings into the air as he tried to adjust to the news. *My parents came over from Austria and if they hadn't they'd be in the thick of it right now. Something has got to be done about it!*

"I still say we could end it all now if we just go and whack Hitler. I could go over to Germany and knock off the bastard myself!"

Lansky and Costello exchanged looks of resignation. They had heard variations on this particular theme many times over the last five years. What even Lansky did not yet know was that Costello had recently been approached by the FBI with a proposal to provide one of the Syndicate's gunmen as part of a plot to assassinate Hitler.

In an attempt to change the subject and cover his own uncertainty Costello instead talked about the raid on the Nazi meeting the previous evening.

"That thing you did last night — it took a lot of guts. I'd be happy to let you have my people go with you to help. Even up the numbers a bit."

"Thanks, but we're doing okay. At least for the time being we want to keep this an all Jewish operation."

They chatted for a while before Lansky left but even his departure did not stop Siegel from returning to the subject of killing Hitler. Gazing at Costello after his friend had gone he tried once more to get him to go along with his plans. He was still choking with rage, longing to take an explosive revenge upon the world in general, and Hitler in particular. He had tried repeatedly to win his friend over but every time he raised the subject Lansky kept telling him an assassination would never work.

"Tell me, you think there's any way we could whack Hitler?"

Costello gazed at him with a neutral expression on his face. Siegel was too useful to the Syndicate to treat him disrespectfully but his obsession with Hitler had begun to irritate some of the non-Jewish members. Until now he'd always told him that some things were beyond even the power of the Mafia to organize and that killing Hitler was one of them. Now he had been approached by the US government and asked to provide a gunman to do just that.

"I know you hate the guy but he's so well protected you'd never get close. But I'll think about it and if you find a good plan let me know. In the meantime I got a date with a Broadway showgirl."

Costello left the table. His handmade shoes were immaculate as ever, his silk shirt without a visible crease showing, and his suit fitted him perfectly with an easy and understated elegance. The proprietor made a sign to a staff member who immediately came across and helped Costello into his cashmere overcoat before handing him his Fedora hat.

Siegel finished his meal and wandered off to think his dark thoughts alone. *Now Austria had fallen who would be next on Hitler's list? Czechoslovakia, perhaps, or maybe Poland.* In the mood he was in right now the last thing he felt like doing was getting drunk or visiting one of his many girlfriends. No, he decided, it was time to go back to his wife Esta and their two young daughters Millicent and Barbara.

Before returning home he visited a florist and bought the largest bouquet of flowers in the shop. He took a cab and, after giving the driver a large tip, entered his apartment.

"Hi, honey. Got something for you."

His wife Esta emerged from the living room and he was startled by her appearance. Her long black hair was styled in the latest fashion with the new cold wave perm. It framed her face which emphasised her artfully applied make-up with pencil thin eyebrows and full pink lips. Her dress was new, shorter than usual and it showed off her slim legs. Made of fine pink wool crepe it was moulded to her body and had padded shoulders. The dress fell softly into pleats and the effect of her latest style was to make her look even more attractive and sexy in his eyes. He hugged her and tried to caress her body, but she pulled away.

"So you come home at last I see. Two whole days I was waiting for you! Where you been, with one of your fancy pieces?"

"No, Esta. Hey, I got you flowers."

"You think I'm blind? So where you been? And what's her name?"

"Hey, it's not a broad, I swear to you. I had to go out and take care of something."

She turned away in disgust.

"Take care of something! Don't you mean someone? How do you think I feel knowing I got two young kids to bring up? Every time you go out I wonder if the next time I get to see you will be at the funeral parlour inside a casket. You even know you *got* two daughters?"

He stared at her in astonishment. It was true that sometimes his wife was moody and unhappy but this was the first time she had ever launched into him with such an outburst.

"Okay, you want to know where I've been the last two days? We went out and smashed up a Nazi meeting in the hall. So that's where I was. After the fight I checked into a hotel, had a bath and slept. Next day I had lunch with Meyer and Frank. And then I came home."

Her eyes filled up with tears, but many of them were tears of pride. She walked across to her husband and took the flowers out of his hand.

"Benjamin Siegel, I swear I don't know what I see in you sometimes. You're the stupidest, most irresponsible man I've ever known! But every now and again I just can't help loving you!"

She kissed him on the cheek and moved towards the kitchen.

He looked at her with a hangdog expression on his face.

"I can't help what I am. But you and my girls mean everything to me."

"I know that. Let's spend some time together before I lose you again."

He spent that night and the next few nights at home with his wife and family, being the dutiful husband and father. For a few brief days Benny Siegel could almost have passed for a respectable family man.

5

One fateful day everything changed as the happy, relaxed man, playing with his two young daughters and being attentive to his wife, vanished instantly.

Siegel was sitting comfortably in his armchair reading the *New York Times* when his gaze became fixed on a news item that read "Hitler to visit Italy." Feverishly he read the news which was only a frustratingly small paragraph stating that he would be making a State visit to Italy at the beginning of May. Siegel sat bolt upright as he digested the information. His eyes stared into space as he became lost in deep thought. The world outside hardly existed as he brooded on this new development.

"You all right?"

"Shut up, I'm thinking."

His brain was working in overdrive as he considered the news. His immediate reaction was of course pure anger — the thought of that monster being welcomed by Mussolini as if he was just like any other leader made him mad with rage. He began to wonder if he could turn the news to his advantage and somehow realize his dream of killing Hitler.

It was still only February so there was plenty of time to organize a plan for the assassination. Siegel began visualizing the scene in his mind. *I've been to Rome a few times and I know the city reasonably well. I could make it happen there — but I'm going to need some help to set up contacts with the Italian Mafia.*

Burning with excitement he wanted to share his new angle on an old idea. Picking up the phone he gave Costello a call.

"Frank? I got a plan I need to run by you."

"Let's meet up. The usual place."

That morning both met in a bar to talk things over. Breathless at the thought of action at last, he laid out his plan in some detail.

"Frank, I need your help setting up the Italian end."

"No problem. I'll use my contacts over there."

"I'm gonna knock off Hitler when he sets foot in Rome."

What a stroke of luck, thought Costello. He knew that the idea of assassinating Hitler had been one of his friend's obsessions for a long time. And now that the Feds had asked him to get one of his own people to help kill Hitler the timing was perfect. Costello considered the plan more carefully, realizing that he'd need to talk it over with the FBI and warn them about their prospective partner in crime.

"In Italy it might be possible to do it. Leave it with me; I'll talk to some people and see if I can get things set up for you."

For a moment Siegel was lost in a world of dreams, caught up in a sudden vision of Hitler lying dead at his feet from a bullet he had fired himself. *For such a sight I could die happy.*

After they parted the idea of assassinating Hitler continued to haunt Benny Siegel's mind He had no choice but to leave the matter in his friend's hands for the time being. No one else had better contacts in Italy than he did and no one else could open doors that would be closed to him otherwise. If anyone could make it happen it would be Frank Costello.

6

Costello met Jones and quickly put the agent in the picture.

"I've got you a shooter but there might be a problem with him."

"What kind of a problem?"

Neither man trusted the other and Jones was already wondering if he was trying to find some way to wriggle out of the situation. Costello was torn by a mixture of emotions; fear for the safety of a man who he genuinely saw as a friend, anxiety that Siegel was so incapable of working with anyone else that he'd screw up the whole mission and a growing awareness of how much was at stake for his country.

"He's rather excitable. Unstable, even. He might be difficult to train and he won't take orders from anyone."

"Do I know him?"

"Yes. His name is Benjamin Siegel."

The FBI man stared at him in genuine shock. He certainly hadn't expected to have him as a co-assassin.

"Bugsy Siegel? I'm impressed. I was expecting one of your foot soldiers."

"Don't ever call him that or he'll kill you. But he's been sounding off at me for the last couple of years about whacking Hitler and when he heard the Germans had marched into Austria he raised it with me again. This time I told him I'd think it over."

Jones gave him a cool stare.

"Well, he's wanted for quite a few murders already so I suppose he's had plenty of practice at killing people. And this time round he might even find some people who felt a bit of sympathy for what he'd done."

"He'd certainly make a credible assassin. Known for his hatred of Hitler and having spoken about killing him quite a few times people would believe he could do it."

"We'd better introduce him to our agent and see what he says. If he thinks he is capable of being trained up as his partner in crime then we'll okay his presence on the team."

They parted and Costello waited for Jones to contact him and make the introductions between Siegel and the real sharpshooter. *If it works, he thought, Hitler will be killed in a government hit but all the suspicion will fall on Benny. I just hope they're not setting him up for a fall. This Federal agent does the killing but Benny takes the blame as a known gangster and gets hung out to dry.*

7

Knowing how much was at stake and that even if his plan did come off it might still be a one-way ticket to Italy, Siegel became particularly attentive to his wife and children. He showered them with gifts, took them out to fancy restaurants and Broadway shows, allowing none of his many girlfriends near him. Esta was delighted with his attentiveness but knew that it was only a temporary phase; eventually he would leave to carry out yet another of his "jobs." It's so hard to love you, Benny, she thought sadly, but it's impossible *not* to love you.

A week passed before Costello called him. He knew at once what was coming. Lansky would be at the meeting as well and they would discuss the plan. With a mounting sense of excitement he prepared for his date with destiny.

"I got to go out, Esta. Meeting Meyer and Frank. I'll be back but I might have to go away for a while pretty soon."

Her eyes filled with sadness when he said that. She'd always known that sooner or later he'd go out on another of his "jobs" but the last few days had been a time of great happiness for her. Benny had been charming, funny, caring and considerate and she loved him so much when he was like that. Now he was off on yet another commission to kill. She shivered as she reminded herself of the dark side of her husband, the side she'd been able to forget completely for the last few days.

"I always feel like I only ever get a part of you. I'm just glad at least it's the *good* part."

A rare twinge of guilt swept through him.

"I'm not sure when I'll be gone but I'll be back later today. You can count on it."

On his arrival at the rendezvous Siegel noticed at once that as well as Costello and Lansky another man was also present, one he had never seen before.

"This is Luigi Carmona. He's someone we use for specialist jobs. Luigi, this is Benny Siegel."

Siegel was impatient to get down to business and was still unsure about the newcomer.

"What do you think about the plan we discussed, Frank?"

"I gave it a lot of thought. That's where Luigi comes in. He's the man who could make it happen for us."

Siegel, intrigued by that remark, gazed at Carmona curiously. He saw a man much older than himself, perhaps late forties or early fifties, with a wiry frame, not much hair on his head but with penetrating brown eyes that gave the impression they were constantly scanning him. He was certainly not the type of man he had expected to meet.

"What are you looking at me for? I don't even know you!"

"I don't know you either," Carmona said.

"How do you know Frank and Meyer?"

"Business.'

"Meyer and I talked your idea over plenty," Costello said, trying to avoid awkward questions. "It's got real possibilities but it needs a few changes."

"Sure, I always figured it might. What kind of changes?"

"You'll never get close enough to Hitler to kill him with a handgun. The only way it could work is from a distance with a high powered rifle. That's where Luigi comes in."

Siegel looked downcast when he heard the news. *I just thought I'd be standing over that punk Hitler and squeezing the trigger. I know guns. I could shoot a pistol in my sleep. But a rifle's different. Frank's taken my idea but it's going to be Luigi grabbing all the glory instead of me.*

"I can see the idea," Siegel said, an edgy tone to his voice as he felt himself beginning to get excited. "But you know me. I always like to go on a hit even if I'm not the main shooter. And this is Hitler we're talking about, right! I really want to be in on the kill. I could learn to use a rifle. I could be there in Italy and pull the trigger. It can't be that much different than a revolver or automatic."

Both men looked at one another before replying. They knew his nature and were prepared for this reaction.

"Benny, nobody said you couldn't go on this mission. But Luigi is an expert shot. He served in the Italian army during the war before he emigrated to the US and was one of the best snipers they had. If anyone can take out Hitler, he can. He's Italian so he speaks the language; he can move about freely over there which you can't, and he's got contacts in the country which you don't. He's the ideal man to have as the main shooter in the enterprise but of course you'll be joining him and you'll have just as much chance of killing Hitler as he will."

Siegel's face brightened up when he heard that.

"So I still get to go?"

"Sure you do. We know how much you want this."

Lansky had been quiet up to now but when he spoke his words devastated Siegel.

"Luigi will be in charge on this mission."

"It was my idea and I even drew up the plan to whack the bastard!"

Siegel stared right into Carmona's eyes with suspicion.

"I've been in the rackets a long time now. How come I never heard of you?"

"That's because I've never been caught."

"Meaning what?"

"If you're good enough at your job you don't get caught."

"So what is your job?"

"I rob banks. That's why I'm so good with a rifle."

Costello spoke up again.

"We know Luigi and he's the best we've got for this particular job. Let's get back to the business in hand."

"But I'm a Jew. It ought to be one of our people knocks him off."

Carmona, who had said nothing throughout these exchanges, made his presence felt. Looking straight at Siegel he spoke with a firm authority that surprised the gangster.

"I'm a Jew. I want this as much as you do."

Siegel stared at the older man in astonishment, not expecting that confession at all. He gazed at the three of them, silent for once.

Costello decided to steer the discussion back on track.

"We've got every confidence in both of you, Benny. Meyer and me have talked this over a lot and putting Luigi in charge gives us the best chance of making it work. It's nothing personal. It's just business. You can understand that, right?"

Carmona tried to reassure Siegel, realizing how unenthusiastic he was about playing second fiddle on this mission.

"It was your idea, Benny, and I'll train you. Hitler won't arrive till the start of May so we've got a few weeks. I could take you up country with me, show you how to use a rifle and turn you into a proper marksman. Two shooters give us a better percentage than just one guy. We'll pick a vantage point and shoot him dead with concentrated fire."

"Let's see how you make out in training, Benny," said Lansky.

"I'll be fine. Why wouldn't I be?"

Lansky said nothing but stole a glance at Costello reminding both of the discussion they'd had about Siegel. *Frank thinks Benny can do it but I'm not so sure. All the things that make him such a good hit man for normal jobs could make him a liability for a mission where stealth, concealment, patience, precision and ingenuity are what you need. Benny's used to just breezing in all guns blazing; in Italy that will just mean he winds up dead.*

There was also got the extra complication of Luigi Carmona. A government man. How could they be sure they could trust him? Carmona had his own agenda and Benny was just the cover. It would be Carmona who

36

killed Hitler if it could be done at all. Would he throw Benny to the wolves when the job was done?

They thought they could take Benny's aggression and courage and channel it but could they really get him to be patient and calm rather than lashing out at the first thing? All they could do was hope.

8

There was a curious undercurrent of melancholy in Carmona's heart, an inner conflict between the man he was now and the person he used to be. In Italy he had worked as a craftsman in Rome but with the outbreak of the First World War found himself in the Italian army fighting for king and country.

When the war was over at last Italy no longer needed his services. His skills were now less in demand with an increasingly industrialized Italy and he struggled to make a living. Unemployment was high with the return of peace and then Mussolini came to power. Carmona hated fascism and that was the beginning of a new phase in his career. He became involved with anti-fascist resistance groups and carried out a number of activities ranging from planting bombs to sabotage. After a while Italy became too dangerous for him as the fascists cracked down ruthlessly on opposition and he reluctantly decided to emigrate.

He chose to make his way to America where he struggled at first before his skills in combat and shooting came to the attention of the authorities. From that moment his life changed as he was recruited to work for American intelligence. This time round he had been asked to work with the leaders of organized crime in America — the Syndicate, as its members referred to it — and found himself liaising with the Mafia Don Frank Costello.

Carmona remembered the day he was summoned to a meeting by his field officer. It was a week before he met Costello and Lansky and ten days before he first met Siegel. Two other men were present at the meeting and he had never seen either of them before. One was obviously a very senior intelligence officer and the other seemed to be some kind of political adviser. Of course neither man gave his name or said exactly what he was.

The advisor spoke first and explained that the international situation was much more dangerous now that Hitler was pursuing an aggressive foreign policy.

"It can't go on," the adviser said. "Sooner or later it's going to mean war. You know what that means and we have to do everything in our power to stop it."

Carmona said nothing, simply sitting, listening and evaluating the information. It was obvious that he was going to be asked to undertake some sort of mission to try and prevent a new world conflict but it was not immediately clear to him how he could do that. Then the other man addressed him.

"Luigi, you've had a good record with us. We also know about your wartime service in Italy and your specialist skills could be invaluable to us. There's no doubt in my mind you're the right man for this job but for a number of reasons we can't ask you to operate alone."

The man stopped speaking for a moment and took off his glasses to clean them. Carmona sensed that he was reluctant to continue with the briefing and was intrigued. He finished cleaning his glasses and finally spoke again.

"The thing is we can't send another agent with you. You'd have to be working with a representative of organized crime."

That announcement surprised Carmona and made him even more curious about exactly what type of mission they had in mind for him. The other man looked impatiently at his colleague and decided to move proceedings along. Carmona guessed that he was probably from the State Department.

"Let's cut to the chase," he said, almost glaring at the intelligence officer. "We want you to assassinate Hitler."

Even the normally phlegmatic Carmona was surprised when he heard that piece of news. He had certainly not expected to be given an assignment like that

"I see," he said after he had fully digested the information. "When and where?"

The man from the agency looked at Carmona hesitantly but the adviser had clearly decided there was no point in prevarication.

"Hitler will be paying a state visit to Italy in May. That is when you will kill him. Where and how are questions I think you'll be better able to judge when you're on the spot."

"I understand."

"Now in case you're wondering why we want you to work with the mob I'll tell you. The order for this — mission — comes direct from the highest authority in the land."

Carmona stared at him in astonishment and could hardly believe his ears.

"You mean the President?"

The adviser did not answer but his silence was clear enough to Carmona.

"Of course you understand that they're can't be any possible connection between the assassination of Hitler and the US government or any representative of it. That's why you'll be working with a professional gangster. Our intention is to make it look like a Mafia killing."

Carmona took in that piece of news and on reflection was not surprised but could see immediate difficulties in making that story plausible.

"It's a good idea but why would the Mafia want to kill Hitler? They've got no reason to want him dead."

"That's a point we've already considered. Now we've liaised with the most senior representatives of the Syndicate in the United States and discussed that very issue with them. Of course they know that the true target is Hitler but in order to gain the co-operation of the Mafia in Italy we'll be using a cover story. The version they'll be told is that the intended victim is Mussolini."

Carmona saw the logic of that suggestion immediately. Ever since he took power in Italy Mussolini had cracked down hard on the Mafia and put many of its leaders in prison. The idea that the Mafia would want him assassinated was certainly a plausible one.

"Have you found a partner for me?"

"We're leaving that up to the Syndicate. Your cover story will be that you are a bank robber and that's how it has to stay. There's no way you can risk letting the truth come out."

"I understand. What about — well, back-up? In case something goes wrong and we get arrested? Or something equally unexpected happens to throw the plan off course?"

The adviser gave him a cold look when he asked that question.

"You're on your own on this mission if anything goes wrong. Anything at all. We can't allow it to be traced back to the US government. You'll have to improvise and hopefully if everything goes to plan Hitler will be dead and we won't be facing the threat of another world war."

Carmona gazed briefly at the two men from the agency. The more senior one looked embarrassed and angry by the whole business but Carmona's supervisor gave him a sad glance. He was dismissed shortly after and prepared to await further instructions. Later his field officer had a quiet word with him. Carmona listened attentively and with considerable surprise to what he had to say.

"Luigi, the guys you saw today are — well, political operators, you could say. All they care about is not letting the world know the US government wants Hitler dead. They don't give a rat's ass about the welfare of our agents. In their eyes you're nothing but a tool they use to get a job done. But I've known you a few years now, so I'm going to stick my neck out on this one and see to it you get some — unofficial help when you're in Rome. I'll give you a contact number to call in an emergency and a man will respond. If need be he's also got two other people he can call on to help you escape after you've carried out the assassination."

Carmona was overcome with a mixture of astonishment and genuine gratitude. He'd already mentally resigned himself to a lonely vigil with no prospect of assistance in case things blew up in his face but now his boss was offering a helping hand.

"I don't know what to say. I didn't expect that at all."

"Just don't let anyone else find out about it. And make sure you kill the bastard!"

"He's a dead man walking."

Now that he had met Siegel he saw a number of problems with the plan. *They want me to assassinate one of the most high profile leaders in the world and to train up some gangster so he can take the rap. The guy I'm working with is hot-headed, impatient, and volatile and he doesn't know one end of a rifle from another. And I have to pretend to be a professional criminal like him rather than a government man. None of the job is easy but working with a Mafia lout will be the hardest part of the whole mission. I wish he wasn't such a loose cannon but I'm stuck with him. All I can do is hope I can train him up and we kill Hitler.*

9

Esta Siegel did not recognize the two men who came to her door the day after her husband's meeting in the hotel suite but she knew at once they had come for her husband and they looked like trouble. The man in charge smiled at her pleasantly enough.

"Got a message from Frank," he said. "Benny needs to leave town for a few days. Tell him to wait in the hotel lobby; he knows which one."

"How soon?" Esta asked, trying to keep the anger and fear out of her voice.

"An hour from now; no later."

"Should I pack a suitcase?"

"He'll be travelling light."

"How long will he be gone?

"A week, maybe two."

"Can I contact him?"

The man looked at her with an expression of sympathy but shook his head.

After the men had left Esta sat down and cried. *Not again, she thought angrily; yet another dirty gangster that Benny has to go and murder. And why a week? Or even more? Where the hell was he going that would take so long? Anywhere in America, even California or Hawaii, he'd be back sooner than that.*

10

Later that afternoon Benny Siegel said a tearful farewell to his wife and left for his latest mission. Carmona took him in a truck with two other men and Siegel's two bodyguards. They drove upstate from New York City and headed north. The atmosphere was tense but Carmona tried to relax his unwanted guest as much as possible.

Climbing the long hilly roads, the truck made its way slowly towards inland Massachusetts. There was still snow on the ground and the trees were bare rather than in bloom as the whiteness of the snow rested upon them like a scarf of cold but Siegel still saw the innate beauty of the landscape. Most of his time was spent in cities and the countryside was something he passed through occasionally on his way to another city, another contract. Now for a week or so he would live within its stillness, its isolation and almost overpowering sense of calm.

The truck moved purposefully into the rural western part of Massachusetts until finally it turned off down a dirt track before coming to a stop outside a newly built log home. It was early evening and the darkness was beginning to close in upon them.

"Well, Benny, this is home for the next week or two. We've fixed it up pretty good and I hope you'll enjoy your time in my place."

"Yeah, nice place you got here. I think I just might enjoy my vacation. You come up here sometimes to go hunting, right?"

"Yes. And that's what we're going to be doing for probably the next two weeks. This won't be a vacation. You're here to watch, to listen, to learn and to work. I'll show you how to fire a rifle from different angles and positions, get you in shape and alter your appearance. So let's start moving. Frankie, get some logs and start up a fire. The rest of you guys get everything out of the truck and bring it inside."

While the others were busy the two of them wandered around the house. It had been built only five years previously to modern specifications but had a rustic, cosy charm about it. A huge stone fireplace dominated the lounge where sofas and plumped-up cushions were placed for the comfort of the guests. The red cedar floors were covered with colourful rugs and one wall was covered with a bookshelf. There was even a games room with a pool table. The log home would clearly be a comfortable place to stay.

"This is your room. I've fixed you up with one on the second floor. Take a look out the window; the view stretches for miles. Nobody lives round these parts so we won't be disturbed. If you want you can practise target shooting from out of the windows."

"I guess I'll have to try all sorts of different ways to get my shooting right."

"Tomorrow I'll set up special markers at different distances for you to aim at so you can fire from several positions. You can lay down on the roof if you want; that trap door over there leads up to it."

"I'll try anything that helps."

"Frankie's gonna fix us some food now. If you want to get cleaned up first go right ahead. We'll be eating in about a half hour."

He was about to turn and leave when a thought struck him.

"I need you to grow a moustache. So don't shave your upper lip, right? Remember we need you to look different in the photo we'll be using on your phoney passport."

Siegel stared at him in horror.

"You want I grow a tash? No way!"

"Ah, come on, you'll look just like Errol Flynn. Anyway, the whole point is so you don't get recognized."

"Maybe, but."

Siegel was torn between his vanity and the realization that Carmona's suggestion made sense. In the end he just shook his head sadly.

"I'll do it. But I'm not growing a beard."

"A moustache will do just fine. Well, see you later. Here's your room. If you need some warm clothes or extra blankets just help yourself. You'll find them in the cupboard over there. "

Siegel prepared to make himself up for the evening meal. Carmona went downstairs and chatted to the four men who had accompanied him. Two, Frankie and Rocco, were Costello's people; the other two were Siegel's bodyguards.

The two Jews, Harry "the Weasel" Levin and Morris "Goldie" Goldstein had worked for Siegel for the last six years and were regarded as among the most reliable and dangerous gangsters in the business. Both men were possessed of immense physical strength and had frequently gone out with him on "jobs."

Carmona sat down, his eyes constantly darting around the room, his ears straining attentively to catch the slightest sound. There was always an air of intense concentration about him even when he was still and silent.

He had been evaluating his partner from the moment they first met. It was immediately obvious to him that he found difficulty in controlling his temper, lacked patience and was far too arrogant for his own good. On the other hand his dedication, ruthlessness, strength and courage were unquestionable. *If only I could get him to bring himself under control he just might be able to pull it off,* *he thought.*

Frankie, well aware that three of the party were Jewish (he did not know that Carmona was also a Jew), asked Levin and Goldstein if they'd eat hot dogs. Both men gave their assent and then he asked about Siegel. A faint smile crossed Levin's face as he answered that question.

"It ain't exactly what he has most days, but he'll eat it. Got anything else?"

"Burgers, onions, not much else right now. Tomorrow will be better, though. It's just the first night and there's not much on offer."

Carmona sat listening to the stillness outside. Although he had grown up in Rome and had long since adapted to life in New York City there remained a part of his nature that sometimes craved for the countryside. The log home was his private retreat from the bustle and conflict of the metropolis.

Siegel came downstairs when the meal was ready. He was no longer dressed in his immaculate but gaudy clothes. Now he wore costume more suited to the hunting trip that was the cover story for the group in case any strangers stumbled upon them inadvertently.

Frankie opened six bottles of beer and passed them around to go with the burgers and hot dogs. As they sat around the table and ate Carmona studied Siegel intently. Right now he seemed relaxed enough but they hadn't even started on his training yet. *Once he's been shut away in silence and isolation for a few days, frustrated at how long it will take him to master a sniper's rifle, that will be the real test. Can he cope with the boredom, the confinement, the endless practice for hour upon hour, the slow progress he'd inevitably have to make? Can he handle all that and come through it a properly trained sniper or will he crack up under the strain? Only time will tell.*

Carmona knew that the next ten days would be gruelling both physically and psychologically. *The whole way he moves, positions his body, even how he thinks all have to be radically transformed and brought under control. There are so many factors that came into play with shooting and so little time in which to prepare him for them.*

As darkness fell and the men retired to sleep only the sound of a gushing river could be heard along with the occasional call of a coyote disturbing the overwhelming silence of the landscape around the log home.

When Siegel rose from sleep on his first full morning in the log home he felt good. He found the idea of spending two weeks away from the constant noise and traffic of New York City a refreshing change. Even the crisp fresh air that filled his lungs seemed to give him renewed energy. There were just the six of them and he felt free from the pressure and constant activity that seemed almost to surround you physically in New York.

He gazed out of the window at the birds flying from the trees and thought for a moment how simple their lives were. A couple of rabbits scampered across the frozen earth before disappearing back into their warrens. *It's a different world out here in the country, Siegel thought. Maybe I could get to like it in time.*

After breakfast they went outside and he watched Carmona setting up markers. He picked up a rifle and looked at it with the practiced eye of a professional sharpshooter.

"This," he said, "is a variant of the German Mauser. It's called the Karabiner 98 Kurz which in English means —"

"I know what it means. My parents spoke German, for God's sake. It means 'carbine 98 short.' Just teach me how to use it!"

He ignored his outburst and continued to speak about the weapon.

"The 98K is the most advanced and sophisticated rifle in the world. The German Army uses it and they've even developed a model specially adapted for snipers which of course is what we are. You can load cartridges one at a time but I think it's better if we load five rounds from a stripper clip into the magazine instead. It has a turned down bolt handle which means it's much quicker to fire.

You've got an open post sight at the front and a tangent sight at the rear with a V-shaped rear notch. These sighting features make it ideal for aiming at targets in the distance which of course we will be. The telescopic sight on the sniper model we'll be using gives us a range of a thousand meters — that's nearly 1100 yards. Oh yes, it's also got a silencer but we won't be using that just yet."

He showed him the gun and hoped he'd taken in at least some of what he'd just told him.

"This is it, the latest thing, It's the most modern sniper rifle there is."

He picked up the Karabiner 98K and handed it to Siegel.

"Here you are, your very first lesson in how to fire a rifle. I'm going to start by showing you how to load it. Then we'll see if you can hit that marker."

As the barrel glinted in the weak sun, its gleaming metal reflected briefly in the window behind them. Momentarily Siegel was startled but immediately realized what it was and relaxed.

After he'd taken his first few shots Carmona shook his head and tried to get him to improve his posture.

"You're not standing right. Put the rifle butt tight up against your shoulder. Don't try to fire it like a pistol. It's not the same sort of weapon at all."

The weather was wet and chilly as the snow slowly began thawing under the pale sun. Flurries of snow made shooting difficult. Over and over again that morning they practised loading, cleaning, disassembling and reassembling the rifle. Carmona tried hard to be patient but Siegel was anything but an easy pupil — not least because he lacked patience and kept getting his shooting positions wrong.

"Hell, I never thought it would be any different using a rifle."

"Just remember the three points I've shown you. They're totally crucial to good marksmanship. Now tell me again what they are."

Siegel looked up wearily from his shooting position and thought for a moment.

"Before I begin shooting I have to make sure the sights are properly adjusted and that my rifle will shoot where it's pointed. I got to breathe right and control the trigger and then I squeeze the trigger. Christ, you'd think I'd never used a gun before!"

Days of endless target practice using different positions was the routine including hunting in the woods and at moving targets. They ate well on the spoils with a turkey, pheasant, partridges and even a white-tailed deer on the menu all of which were turned into gourmet meals.

Siegel controlled his drinking and only allowed himself a single Bourbon after the evening meal. He relaxed by playing a game of pool or exercising with the weights in the gym before retiring early to bed after a tiring day.

For three days Carmona drilled Siegel relentlessly. He practised his breathing, sighting the rifle and trying to hit moving targets. After he had spent a few days in the vastness of Massachusetts with its endless trees and scrub the feeling of wonder he had experienced at first disappeared entirely. A growing sense of isolation, the oppressive silence and the total absence of activity began to overpower him. He never saw another car, a shop or even another human being besides Carmona and the other bodyguards. He became numb, his emotions as frozen as the winter weather around him and he became more and more depressed by the absence of the familiar things that he experienced on a daily basis back in New York.

At the slightest problem he flared up and was close to breaking point. He was inside a closed world with nothing at all to anticipate or look forward to beyond the relentless firing of the rifles. There was no point in dressing for dinner or adding up how much money he had made that day. His world felt like a prison and the countryside like a desert island on which he was stranded until rescue finally came. *God, how can I possibly stand two whole weeks of this? I only know that I have to and there's no escape for me until the job is done.*

Carmona saw the mental state that he was in and allowed Siegel a couple of Bourbons in the evening to relax him. He also played cards or pool to try to dispel the growing depression that was making him increasingly irritable and listless. One moment he hardly had the energy to get out of bed and the next he was shouting at people for no reason.

At one point the slow progress he was making became so intolerable to Siegel that he was on the point of giving up.

"Luigi, I just can't do it. I'll never get the hang of this damn thing!"

He threw the rifle on the ground on to the soft snow and stood up, waving his arms about. Carmona picked up the gun and checked that it was not damaged before wearily trudging after him. He was already disappearing towards the log home, his feet crunching on the snow that still lay on the ground. Carmona wondered for a moment if he should just give up the whole idea of training him. *It isn't just the technical difficulties of teaching him how to shoot a rifle. We can overcome that with time. What's far harder to come to terms with is his attitude.*

"Benny! Let's stop and talk about it. You want to go through with this or not?"

Siegel stopped his sullen trudge through the snow and turned around. He stared at the advancing figure of Carmona with open hostility.

"Yeah, I want to do it. But I'm sick of you treating me like I was some kid in school. I'm Benny Siegel and in my world people respect me and they're scared of me. Out here I feel totally useless!"

"I know it's frustrating, tedious and time-consuming learning to use a rifle properly. Do you think I didn't curse, swear, and want to give up when I was learning? Do you think I wasn't drilled for weeks before I finally got it right? My country was at war and I had to do it. Just like we are now, I was motivated. Don't you want to blast that bastard Hitler to hell with your own hands? Come on, it's all going to fall in place soon enough."

Siegel nodded, still fuming but realizing he either had to pull out of the mission completely or persevere with his training.

"I sure hope so. I'm sick of all this practising. The sooner I can get out of here the better I'll feel."

The days passed and slowly Siegel began to improve his shooting. By the time two weeks had passed

Carmona's constant drilling had succeeded in turning him into a competent marksman. With considerable relief they left the hunting lodge and returned to New York City. *I know who I am, thought Siegel, a city boy from New York. I love the crowds, the noise and living on the edge. It was interesting staying in the country but there's no way I'm going through that again. Fine place to visit for a day or two but I couldn't stand living there!*

Even on his return to familiar turf his troubles were not over. Carmona went to see Costello and they discussed the next phase of their plans. Costello began by asking Carmona about the tempestuous fortnight in the lodge.

"Did it go off all right? No major problems?"

Carmona hesitated for a moment but then decided he would not be doing anyone any favours if he held back on the downside of the events.

"You want an honest answer, Frank?"

"Of course."

"Well, he is without a doubt the most reckless, irresponsible, ill-disciplined and unreliable man I've ever had to train. But we got there in the end. He can handle a rifle okay."

"Well enough to hit our target?"

"Yes, I think so. Of course I'm worried he might go off half-cocked and jeopardize the plan. Not that I think he will but he's not good at just waiting patiently for the quarry to come into sight."

"Yeah, he doesn't much like waiting up on things. Now let's run through the plans. You and he will travel to Naples on phoney passports and once you've cleared customs and immigration you'll be met by a car. That will take you to a safe house on the outskirts of Rome where you'll meet Don Mancini. He's our contact in the city and he'll set up the weapons and anything else you need. He'll give you the itinerary and routes of Hitler's trip so you can study them and work out when you've got the best opportunity to kill him. The Don will also provide you with transport out of the city and on to a fishing boat that will drop you off in the Mediterranean where you'll transfer to a freighter. It will take you back to America and then you can go back to your old life."

Carmona was already mentally planning the operation and devising a sequence of events in his head.

"You know, even if we get away with it they won't know who killed him."

"We'll know, Luigi."

To finalize plans Costello held a last meeting with the two assassins. At this last planning session before their departure the arrangements for the killing and their getaway were discussed in detail.

"Don't forget, don't let anyone know who the real target is. As far as Don Mancini is concerned our plan is to kill Mussolini. That's why his people have been so eager to co-operate. It might have been harder to persuade them to help us if we told them openly it's Hitler we're after. Don't forget that — under no circumstances talk about killing Hitler. It's Mussolini — always Mussolini. That's our cover story. Got that?"

Both men agreed and each understood the logic behind the instructions. It would be hard enough to carry out the mission successfully as it was and anything that might make it even more difficult had to be avoided. The last thing either of them wanted was to lose the co-operation of Mancini and the Mafia. Without their help it would be almost impossible to carry out the hit successfully.

"You can count on us to remember what you've said, Frank," said Siegel.

His face lit up with excitement as he reflected on how the long and boring and tiring period of training was all going to be worth it. *Soon, he thought, soon I'll be standing somewhere in Rome with a rifle in my hand and squeezing the trigger and sending that bastard Hitler right to hell where he belongs. I can hardly wait!*

11

The *MS Vulcania* left New York bound for the port of Naples. As the ship made its way slowly towards their eventual destination the seemingly unending waters of the Atlantic Ocean provided a monotonous backdrop to their journey into Europe. There was no land in sight to distract their attention from the rolling waves.

There was plenty on board the ship to keep the passengers amused. They could squander lazy happy-go-lucky hours in playing, swimming and sun tanning themselves. Even at night, life still continued in the sumptuous interior of the ship. All the things Siegel liked were on offer – dancing, drinking, gambling and girls. He knew that there was fun to be had and wanted to go down to the ballroom and dance.

"Forget it, Benny. We're not on vacation."

"So what am I supposed to do?"

"Stay in your cabin and keep yourself to yourself. Somebody might recognize you."

Siegel poured himself a large glass of Bourbon and drank it down rapidly. As the fiery liquid rushed to the back of his throat he felt better.

"I wish it was over. I can't stand being cooped up like this. It feels like I'm in prison instead of on board a ship."

"You're going to have to be patient. It'll be worth it in the end. The waiting always gets to you but we can't take any chances. Just stay out of sight as much as possible. Out of sight means out of trouble, remember?"

"Yeah, yeah, I'll remember. It ain't easy, though."

"None of it's easy. Do you think it will be easy when we arrive? Patience, watchfulness and self-control are all we have to give us our best chance so let's make sure we got them. No sense in taking any unnecessary risks."

They spent their time in daily exercise, running around the deck and building up their strength with press-ups in the cabin of the ship. Carmona ate his meals in the restaurant while Siegel dined alone in his cabin. The sheer monotony of keeping a low profile made Siegel extremely agitated, and he became virtually a chain-smoker on the voyage. As the two men were about to begin their daily routine of running Siegel stopped and stared.

His eye rested on two young women sitting in deck chairs and letting the cool ocean breeze play gently upon them. Both were in their early twenties and there was no sign of any other males around. One had blonde hair and a slim figure while the other had jet-black hair and was fuller-figured. Gazing at the two girls with considerable interest Siegel prepared to approach them.

"Hi there," he said, flashing a smile.

The two girls returned his gaze with an almost predatory stare of their own. Their silence seemed almost like a challenge to him and he persisted, not used to being rebuffed by women.

"I'm an American. Where are you girls from?"

The women looked at one another before finally responding. The dark-haired girl answered him first.

"I am Italian, signor."

"And your friend?"

The blonde girl was just about to answer when Carmona came rushing over.

"There you are. Come on, let's get moving!"

He tugged him forward by the arm and reluctantly he let himself be pulled away. As they began running round the deck Siegel cast a regretful glance behind him.

"Two good looking broads like that and you drag me away from them!"

"What did we say about keeping a low profile?"

He stopped running and turned to face Carmona. He raised his fist angrily and then lowered it again.

"Low profile, sure, but I didn't know that meant I had to stay away from girls!"

Carmona waved him to a couple of spare chairs on the deck and they sat down.

"Look, you got to use your head. The more you circulate the more attention you attract. I don't care what you do once this is all over but until then you have to hold it together. And yes, I'm afraid that does mean no chasing girls."

Siegel gazed out at the swirling waters of the Atlantic Ocean as they broke all around the ship.

"The hell with it," he said finally. "I guess I'll just have to wait. Shame, though, they were two good-looking broads."

As they sat there the two girls they had seen earlier walked past. To Siegel's horror they were talking to each other in German.

"Christ," he said as soon as they'd passed out of earshot. "The blonde must be a Kraut. I had a lucky escape there."

Seizing the moment Carmona stood up.

"Let's finish our run around the deck."

After they finished running they returned to the cabin. Siegel turned on the wireless but when the music began playing he wanted to dance. He knew that this time his journey would be grim and pleasureless and the enforced isolation and boredom would drive him crazy. Turning off the wireless, he lay down on his bed and tried to sleep.

"I never realized how hard this part of things was going to be."

He gave a slight laugh as he remembered the scene on deck earlier.

"Those two girls probably think we're a couple of faggots!"

"I'd rather they thought that than found out the truth."

"I guess. Look, I just got mad when you pulled me away. I'll stay out of sight in future."

Once again the unstable personality of Siegel had threatened to put the entire mission at risk simply because of his inability to resist a pretty woman. Not for the first time Carmona wished he had a more reliable accomplice.

***

After a sixteen-day journey the ship docked at Naples where spring had arrived. Carmona felt the warmth of the sun's rays on his face and breathed the air of his native land for the first time in fourteen years. He felt at peace with himself and became convinced that it would be all right in spite of the danger and the additional difficulties posed by his partner. The two men walked off the ship and towards the immigration officer.

Siegel was nervous about being recognized but his changed appearance and the quality of his false passport was good enough. The officer took their documents and looked at them for a moment or two.

"Buon giorno, Signor Rossi, Signor Bradley," he greeted them pleasantly enough. "What is your business here?"

Carmona smiled confidently as both men opened their suitcases.

"We're here to sell nylon toothbrushes," Siegel explained. "It's the latest thing."

Carmona decided to elaborate upon their cover story and as both he and the official were Italian he could avoid any possible misunderstandings through Siegel's ignorance of the language.

"We are distributors for the Du Pont Company in America. Have you heard of their new material nylon?"

"Si, si," the officer said as he examined the sample nylon toothbrushes on display. He also picked up the brochures and price lists and studied them intently.

"I will need to search you both," he said.

"Fine," said Siegel, lifting his arms up.

The officer patted down Siegel over his grey lightweight suit and took off his straw Panama hat. Then he turned to Carmona, patting down his olive-green suit and then at last the process was over.

"You may go through now. I wish you good luck in obtaining many orders."

They were relieved that the first hurdle was over. Once the two of them had left the port Siegel lit up a cigarette and turned to Carmona with a rueful grin.

"I've really come down in the world, Luigi, me, a toothbrush salesman!"

Carmona laughed and felt the tension ease a little.

"I bet it's the only honest job you've ever had!"

"Only idiots work."

Looking around for their contact they saw an old Fiat with two men sitting in the front who motioned to them to come over. A few words in Italian were exchanged and then they entered the car, setting out on the way to Rome.

The two men introduced themselves as they began to drive towards Rome. They discovered that the driver's name was Giovanni Bernardi and the other man was called Alberto Moretti.

"Call us Luigi and Benny," said Carmona.

Siegel glanced at him curiously and wondered why he hadn't given their surnames. After all they were travelling on phoney IDs anyway so what difference did it make? *Sometimes I think Luigi gets too cautious.*

Moretti spoke better English than his companion who in any case was concentrating on driving slowly and discreetly towards their destination. Siegel found Moretti's constant talking an irritation and in the end he just decided to put a stop to it.

"Alberto, we're both pretty tired. Let's just rest up for a while and get our strength back."

They took the coastal road, passing rocky cliffs interspersed with smooth sandy coves. Siegel noticed the swarms of water-birds flying through the stone pines.

"If we had our shooters we could have a field day here."

Carmona agreed and returned to his thoughts.

They drove at a steady pace and two hours later arrived at a modest concrete bungalow on the outskirts of Rome. It was festooned with ivy climbing up the trellis and the garden was awash with flowers. A set of metal gates protected the house from unexpected visitors and as they reached it the driver stopped the car briefly. He pressed a buzzer and the gates slowly opened. The car made its way through and parked in the back yard. Once they were safely inside they entered the back door and went into a cool, dark, comfortable living room.

The furniture was covered with dust-sheets and the floor and every surface was dusty.

"I am sorry for the dust," Bernardi said. "Nobody lives here. We only use this place for business."

In spite of the dustiness, Moretti and Bernardi tried to make them welcome. Both men were fairly short, dark-skinned and had the air of a perpetually crouching tiger. Moretti's eyes darted about the room constantly and he rarely made direct eye contact with anyone. Bernardi seemed more relaxed and his alertness was somehow less off-putting than Moretti's nervous energy.

They removed the dust-sheets quickly and offered them a jug of beer as well as switching on an electric fan. The weather was hot and muggy and Siegel slumped into an armchair, brushing it with his hands to remove the accumulated dust. Sensing a change of mood in his partner, Carmona turned to him.

"What's up?"

"I've been cooped up on a ship for the last two weeks, that's what. Now I've come to this hole with a bunch of peasants who can hardly speak English. Yeah, I'm pretty fed up right now!"

"Just remember why we're here. This is only temporary. If we manage to do what we've come here for it can change the course of history."

"That's the only thing that's kept me going all this time."

"Look, Don Mancini is coming over this evening. I suggest we grab some lunch and try to get some sleep for a few hours. We've got to be upbeat when the Don comes here."

***

Don Mancini arrived at dusk accompanied by a bodyguard. Moretti and Bernardi rushed to greet him. Siegel thought that Moretti behaved like a lap-dog towards Mancini and he found the man's constant fawning on his boss distasteful. He had grown up with the independence of spirit that America nourished and everything about Moretti irritated him.

He was not much more impressed with Mancini who was a man of bulky appearance and a vacant expression, aged about sixty, sweated profusely and constantly mopped his brow with a handkerchief. Siegel was disgusted by his ungroomed appearance, greasy hair and the smell of body odour that filled the room as soon as he entered. *In America, he thought, a Don like Costello would wear expensive clothes and at least smell sweet.* Carmona noticed Siegel's mood and whispered to him quickly.

"This isn't America. Over here it isn't right even for a Mafia chief to show off his status through his clothing or in any other way. Just remember that he is the top Don here and that we need his co-operation for the mission to succeed."

Carmona then turned rapidly to their visitor and immediately showed him the respect to which he was accustomed.

"Don Mancini, we are both very honored to meet you and very grateful for your assistance. Don Costello sends his best wishes and says that you will be amply rewarded for your services."

Don Mancini nodded in acknowledgement. He flicked his fingers and the two henchmen rapidly disappeared into the kitchen and closed the door. It was an enormous relief to Siegel when Mancini dismissed them and he no longer had to listen to Moretti. The three of them sat round a table and Mancini came straight to the point.

"I can now give you the plans for the assassination of Mussolini."

He spat at the name of Mussolini which added further to Siegel's disgust.

"Benny, open a bottle of wine," said Carmona, trying to distract the attention of the Don and calm down his excitable partner before he said or did something stupid. As he went to open the wine Mancini took a notebook out of his pocket.

"Here is the itinerary Mussolini and Hitler will be taking while touring Rome. These are the times they will be appearing in public."

He passed it across the table along with a street map. Carmona grabbed both items quickly.

"As you can see from the list, Hitler arrives on 3 May. On 5 and 8 May he will be travelling with Mussolini to view the navy manoeuvres in Naples. The security there will be too tight for you to be able to whack the Duce there. You only have a few days when it is possible when he is in Rome."

"What about our guns?" asked Siegel.

Don Mancini smiled as he produced two handguns from his jacket and placed them on the table. Siegel's eyes gleamed with joy as he picked up the gun, almost caressing it with his hands. He felt better now, back to his old self. Now he could protect himself! Two boxes of ammunition were also placed on the table and Siegel quickly inserted some into his gun. Carmona then asked about the rifles.

"I'm moving you out of here in two days' time to an apartment in Rome. I'll bring the rifles and ammunition here tomorrow as well as a set of workmen's" clothes and a couple of tool boxes where you can hide the rifles."

They finished the bottle of wine and Siegel was pleasant enough to Mancini. Now that he had a gun securely in his possession he felt much more relaxed. Mancini said his farewells and told them he would return the following day.

12

Carmona generally slept when darkness fell and rose when the sun began to cast its first faint rays of daylight upon the world. He spent much of his time at his hunting lodge following the natural rhythm of the seasons. It brought a sense of inner peace to his often melancholy heart. By contrast Siegel often went to bed late and rose in the afternoon or at least the later stages of the morning. Carmona left him sleeping as he set out early in the morning to catch the bus into the centre of Rome. He was dressed in his suit and Panama hat and carried his briefcase with its sales brochure and samples. Sitting in the bus he stared out of the window, wondering how much Rome had changed since his departure.

As the bus came over the brow of the hill he gazed in awe at the skyline with its golden domes glistening in the early morning sun. *No wonder the ancients called it the caput mundi -the centre of the world. A million people live here now and I can understand why they are drawn to it as if a magnet pulls them into its embrace. I remember clambering over the ruins of the Coliseum as a child and visiting the colourful street markets. They were alive with sparkle and vibrancy. I remember the endless chatter as my parents haggled with the vendors.*

As the bus approached the city centre he sensed a change in the atmosphere. The Romans were no longer as free and easy as they had been. There was a tension in the air and in spite of the magnificence of the modern buildings that now filled the city Carmona felt uneasy. *Yes, Mussolini has made big changes and he has rebuilt Rome with gleaming marble obelisks as dedications to himself. There are grandiose avenues and he has certainly turned Rome into a modern dynamic city.* Carmona heaved a draught of fresh air, hardly able to believe the transformation that lay before him.

As he turned into La Piazza to his horror Carmona saw abundant evidence of the imminent state visit of the German Chancellor. Swastika flags were everywhere and flying alongside the tricolour banner of Italy. Even the buildings of antiquity were draped in huge swastikas.

How dare they hang swastikas side by side with our own flag, he thought angrily? How dare they deface the ancient monuments with Nazi symbols? What has that bastard Hitler done to my city?

Carmona alighted from the bus in a small back street which he remembered from studying the itinerary the previous night would be one down which Hitler and Mussolini would be riding in an open-top car on 6 May at 10.00 on their way to the art gallery.

As he walked through the streets he began thinking ahead. He already knew the itinerary planned for Hitler's stay in Rome and was mentally identifying possible vantage points from which a sniper could attack.

At last he came a to a small, compact street with apartments above shops. If he could manage to get inside one of them he would be able to use a downward position to shoot from a window. The block was on the corner of the street and at first glance looked an ideal location for his plans.

He looked up at the building, taking in every detail with his photographic memory. The apartment block was a superior building that had been constructed at the turn of the century for middle class Roman residents. It was three stories high with sumptuous arcades below, a line of stone arches fronting the shops in imitation of the Romanesque style of architecture. Each apartment had its own balcony and the fascia of the building had plant motifs in Roman red to embellish the design. The roof was red-tiled and one end of it tapered off to a flat roof.

The apartments had a communal entrance but he also knew that each flat inside the building would have its own front door. Staring hard at a window on the third floor with a balcony a sudden sense of excitement filled him. He realized he had found the ideal vantage point for the assassination of Hitler.

He decided to take a closer look at the entrance to the building. The shops below were now open and busy with customers buying their morning papers and cigarettes. He noticed the large wooden entrance door with its elaborate carving and the bells to each apartment. He wandered into the tobacconist below and asked for his favourite brand of cigarettes.

"They look like nice apartments up there," he said casually.

"Yes, they are very nice inside. They have beautiful mezzanine floors."

"Really? I was thinking about making enquiries about renting or buying one. Do they have a porter?"

"No, but most have their own cleaners."

"Do you happen to know the management company? So I could make enquiries about taking one of the apartments?"

"Yes, it's Pescaro and Co on the Plaza."

"You have been most helpful," Carmona said, now having the information he needed to progress further with his wild plan.

Picking up his briefcase he walked to the corner of the block before turning right. He came across a wrought iron gate which by a stroke of good fortune was open as he approached it. It was early morning and the inhabitants of the block were all busily coming or going. He pushed gently on the gate and it opened. Walking a few yards along the path he could see an inner courtyard which most blocks in Rome possessed and which acted as a tiny sanctuary against the blazing sun and the intense stifling heat of the city in summer. It was a shaded area with a large tree in the middle surrounded by bushes and even had a small fountain in one corner. He looked up and noticed the metal stairs leading from each apartment into the courtyard, doubling up as a fire escape.

He found a cafe across the road and sat down. Ordering an espresso coffee he lit up a cigarette and began considering the ramifications of his plan in more detail when the wailing of police sirens broke the air. Their vans had stopped at the end of the street and everyone leapt up from their seats, including Carmona, who left his money for the coffee on the table.

The *carabinieri* jumped out of the vans and rushed into a small garment factory. A few minutes later four men appeared with their hands above their heads. A tall distinguished man about thirty-five years old took charge of the situation. Carmona admired the fashionable style of his dress. He wore a wide neck tie with bold geometric shapes and the shoulders of his dark suit were lightly padded. The outfit was topped with a Homburg hat on his head. *I used to look like that at his age.*

"What's going on?" he asked a bystander.

"Lieutenant Bellini — that's him in the dark suit — has arrested another bunch of the Mafia scum. He does his job well and is very successful at carrying out Il Duce's crackdown on the Mafia."

A cold shiver passed over him in spite of the heat and he wondered if the Mafia safe house where they were staying really was safe after all. His mind began racing. *Should I look for alternative accommodation with no connection to the Mafia?*

He walked hurriedly across the street, not so quickly as to attract attention but swiftly enough to put distance between himself and the police. His brain was working overtime for a solution to the unexpected new problem of Bellini's crackdown on the Mafia. He knew at once that their already daunting task would be much more difficult now. It was time to take precautions in case the operation was discovered. He knew it was risky to make contact at this early stage but doing nothing seemed to him the greater danger.

Wandering over to a public call box he fished out a coin from his pocket and dialled a number. The phone rang at the other end for a full minute before it was answered. There was a silence on the line which Carmona finally broke.

"Buon giorno," he said. "I need to ask a favor."

Another silence followed before a middle-aged man spoke. His gruff New York accent was unmistakable and Carmona sensed his disapproval even over the phone line.

"Why are you calling me?"

"There has been heavy rain and the river may flood. We may need to evacuate people if it gets worse."

"Take no chances. Contact me again when you're sure. Have you got a place to stay in the meantime?"

Carmona thought quickly as he wrestled with the problem before a sudden feeling of calm passed over him. He realized that he had the perfect solution to their difficulties. *I know the place to go, a place I know so well, a place where I have deep roots.*

"Yes, I think so."

"Good. Call me only when you're sure you need help. If there's flooding and you need to evacuate people you can take them to the church nearby with the Caravaggio painting of the Madonna of Loretto in it."

"I know the one."

The phone went dead and Carmona replaced the receiver and gave a faint wistful smile as he prepared for the next stage in his journey. He crossed over a bridge onto the west side of the Tiber and entered Trastavere, the Jewish quarter of Rome. He pulled down his hat to disguise his face and put on a pair of sunglasses to minimise the risk of being recognized. This was his birthplace, the part of Rome where he was brought up and had spent his life until he left Italy altogether. He made his way through a maze of narrow streets where he could reconnect with his past and solve the problem that Bellini's unexpected raid had created.

13

The sights and sounds of Trastavere comforted Carmona as he entered the part of Rome where he had grown up. The smell of cooking, the dirt, even the stench of rubbish, the sight of the alleyways where you could touch one another from the windows opposite, the paint peeling on the neglected buildings and the familiar sight of washing suspended on lines strung across balconies all made him remember his youth in this ancient part of the city.

Trastavere was a working class district, the poorest and most dangerous quarter of Rome. The inhabitants were extremely proud of being Trastaverini and considered themselves the true Romans, claiming descent from the original founders of the city. They spoke a dialect that was peculiar to them and which often made other Italians laugh when they heard it. The people of Trastavere were hasty, passionate and vengeful if crossed.

The houses were piled one on top of the other and had a staircase in the front room that led to the living or sleeping quarters on the first or second floor. Beneath the two-roomed homes stood shops or workshops on the ground floor.

The sun had brought the people out on to the streets, chatting on the corners and filling up the sidewalk cafes that abounded in the district. Everyone seemed to be shouting and the volume of noise made it hard for Carmona to think clearly. Home, he thought for a brief moment before pushing aside the nostalgic thoughts that came into his head.

He made his way through the mediaeval alleys where nothing had changed since his departure. He paused before a house and hesitated for a moment as he gazed up at a balcony. *Am I doing the right thing? Is it really fair to involve my uncle in this business?*

On the right side of the door a decorative case was placed containing a *mezuzah*, a scroll of parchment containing the words of a Jewish prayer. The *mezuzah* was fixed to the door in a vertical position as was the custom among the Sephardic Jews from whom both the inhabitant of the house and his visitor were descended. Before entering the house Carmona kissed the wooden case containing the parchment, mainly for good luck.

He rang the doorbell and from within heard the shuffling footsteps of the seventy-year-old occupant slowly moving towards the door to open it.

"Hello, Uncle Fredo," Carmona said, gazing at the bald man.

The old man stared back at him for a moment and gazed intently into his face.

"Is it you, Luigi?" he said with a trembling voice.

"Yes, Uncle, it's me. I've come all the way from America to visit you."

Fredo gave his nephew a big hug as tears filled his eyes. It had been a long time since he had last set eyes on him although they corresponded regularly and Carmona regularly sent his uncle money from America.

"Are you on your own?" Carmona asked, looking up and down the street.

He took his uncle by the arm and quickly ushered him into the house. They entered a small room that was neat and tidy. The furniture was exactly the same as it had been on the last occasion that Carmona had seen his uncle, some fourteen years ago.

"Sit, sit," said Fredo eagerly, waving him towards an armchair. "Tell me all about America!"

"It's a great country to live, uncle. It's full of opportunities and you've got the freedom to do what you like."

"Freedom? I have almost forgotten the meaning of that word. You spoke of opportunity; what opportunities have you found for yourself in America?"

"I've done pretty well for myself. I started off working in the wood trade and managed to save some money."

"Ah, to be able to save! Why, no matter how economical I try to be at the end of the week I have nothing left!"

"Times are hard, I know. When the depression came I was able to buy land cheap. I set up my own hunting lodge upstate which I let out during the season."

"And does that bring in much money?" his uncle asked doubtfully.

"I make enough. Of course, we're out of the depression now. There are lots of opportunities to make the American Dream come true."

"So you've done well for yourself. But why is it you've never got married?"

"I've been too busy. Of course I've had women but nothing serious. Somehow I just never really found the right one, I suppose."

He felt the cold wind of loneliness blowing over him as he reflected on his isolation. His life in America had been a solitary one and he had often longed to wake up with the warm body of a woman beside him in the morning rather than the chill air of solitude. The thought made him shiver and he felt uncomfortable about discussing the situation any further.

"And how are you, uncle?" he asked, changing the subject.

"Oh, I manage. I've got a small pick-up truck which I use for furniture removals or anything else for that matter. I go to the synagogue every Friday evening like a good Jew and I do a lot of reading and listening to the wireless."

"What do you think about Hitler visiting our country?"

"That man of the hour can go to hell. I don't like him and I don't like what he's doing to our people. It was bad enough when he was forbidding the Jews to teach or be doctors or lawyers but when he told us who we could or couldn't marry — that was shameful. If a Jew and a non-Jew want to get wed that's their business, not the government's. And as for the constant violence against our people by the SA and SS—"

Fredo fell silent and his nephew waited for him to continue.

"The Nazis get thugs to attack our people, loot our shops and businesses, beat us up and even kill us. And what happens if anyone complains? They get arrested and sent to a concentration camp. It's just not right, Luigi. Something has to be done to put a stop to it. And now

Mussolini's become friendly with Hitler it could happen here, God forbid."

"How would you feel if Hitler was assassinated during his visit to Rome?" he asked his uncle, trying to show a calmness in his voice that he was very far from feeling.

"I'd be delighted if —."

Fredo stopped in mid-sentence and stared hard at his nephew.

"Are you trying to tell me something, Luigi?"

"There is a real danger of war. Hitler is a maniac and is trying to bring Mussolini into a full-scale alliance between Italy and Germany. They've already all but destroyed democracy in Spain. Now Hitler has set his sights on Czechoslovakia and he wants Italy's help if it comes to a war with Britain and France. That is what this meeting of the two dictators is all about — preparations for another war."

"Yes, that is true, I can see that. But why are you here, Luigi?"

"President Roosevelt is concerned. The Americans, like every other country, have an intelligence service. My associate and I have been sent here to stop that from happening. We're going to assassinate Hitler."

Fredo sat down abruptly when he heard that news.

"I need a drink. Are you telling me that you're working for American intelligence?"

"Not directly, but sometimes intelligence agencies recruit — freelance operatives — to do particular jobs for them. And right now they want us to kill Hitler and prevent World War Two."

Fredo drank his brandy quickly and rapidly refilled his glass.

"My God, Luigi, do you realize what you just said?"

"Of course. I know it's dangerous but doing nothing is an even greater danger. The death of Hitler will remove the threat of war and maybe even put an end to the persecution of our people in Germany. It's worth the risk, Uncle Fredo."

"Maybe it is but why does it have to be you? Why must you put your life at risk, Luigi?"

Carmona shook his head sadly.

"Why me? I was in the war and we were on the right side last time round. I'm a crack shot, a trained sniper. When I was asked to carry out this mission I didn't hesitate. The thought of putting right the wrongs our people have suffered at the hands of this one man filled me with a burning desire to end them by killing him."

Fredo stared at his nephew and then raised his glass in an ironic toast.

"Just make sure you kill the bastard. And don't get hurt yourself."

Carmona gave a short laugh.

"Well, I survived the war. After that anything seems like a walk in the park."

Fredo looked at his nephew.

"Why have you come here to tell me all this?"

Carmona looked away for a moment and felt a renewed sense of guilt at the enormous imposition he was about to place on his elderly relative.

"This isn't just a social call. Not that it isn't wonderful to see you and of course it would be totally wrong of me to have come to Rome for the first time in years and not see you. But I need to ask you a favor. A big favor."

"I see. I had a feeling there might be a connection between your visit here and what you have told me. What do you want from me?"

"I'd like you to pick up me and ... my associate ... tonight. There will be two of us carrying out the ... the mission and we need a place to stay. We'll stay out of your hair as much as possible, don't worry. Two days maximum and we'll be gone. When our mission is over the world will be a much better place."

An awkward silence fell between them as each struggled to come to terms with conflicting emotions. Fredo felt a mixture of pride, fear and anger. *Why is Luigi mixed up in something like this? It isn't fair to put this burden on me. These agencies have professionals and it should be one of them who does the killing, not an amateur like Luigi.*

Carmona worried that his revelation of the true purpose of their visit to Italy might put his uncle in danger. He also wondered how Siegel would cope with a couple of days in Trastavere. Its homely honest simplicity was the opposite of the life he knew in New York City and in any case his volatile nature was a constant worry. Most of all he was unsure about the feasibility of the mission. Could they really succeed in killing Hitler? And even if they did, was the escape plan really viable?

A sudden image of himself and Siegel lying dead as the carabinieri riddled them with bullets floated unbidden into his mind. He pushed it aside and concentrated on planning. Now that he'd identified what seemed an ideal location he knew that he and Siegel would have to evaluate it properly. Not for the first time he wished he was carrying out the assassination on his own but it was too late to worry about that now.

"So," he said finally, "will you put the two of us up for a couple of nights?"

"You know I will."

13

While Carmona was busy in Rome, Siegel slept. He rose at noon and took a leisurely bath using the oils he had brought with him, shaved and trimmed his now fully-grown moustache. Putting on a clean, crisp white shirt he looked at himself in the mirror and was finally satisfied.

Lunch was served by the two henchmen but when he saw a plate of pasta being put in front of him Siegel was horrified. *Peasant food, he thought angrily as he reluctantly forced to himself to eat it.* He was pleasantly surprised that the spaghetti al vongole tasted much better than he anticipated. The mixture of garlic, tomatoes and clams made him lick his lips and when he had finished he asked for a second helping. The pasta dish was followed by very sweet pastries and coffee.

He went into the living room and switched on the wireless. To his delight the radio was playing Benny Goodman and his band and he began tapping his feet to the beat. He only stopped when Moretti approached him with a smile on his face.

"You've got a visitor, Benny."

Jumping up from his chair, ready to whack anyone who walked in, he quickly reached for the gun in his pocket. Moretti laughed as he saw his reaction.

"Take it easy, this is a present for you from the Don!"

He looked up as a young woman aged about twenty-five years walked into the room. She was typically Italian, dark-haired with dark eyes and full, sensuous lips. The girl wore a tight fitted floral dress which emphasized her voluptuous figure. Siegel eyed her up and down with obvious appreciation.

"Come on, let's dance!"

He turned up the volume on the wireless and grabbed her round the waist. She started laughing as he began twirling her around the room. How good it was to hear her laughter and to feel the warmth of a woman against him. For a moment he thought of his wife Esta and their two daughters and wondered if he would ever see them again before he dismissed the thought and continued to dance.

When they finished dancing he poured out some wine from the bottle and handed her a glass. Taking the bottle in one hand, he took the girl by the other and led her upstairs. She had already left when Carmona returned to the house in the early evening. He burst inside in an agitated state.

"We need to make new arrangements. Something happened today that made me change my mind about staying here."

"What happened?"

"I saw the carabinieri arresting four of our people, that's what. This safe house may no longer be safe for us to stay in. And we daren't jeopardize the whole mission at this stage."

"We'd better tell Don Mancini when he gets here and try to make other arrangements."

"I've already done that. I've been pretty damn busy today working out all the fine tuning for the plan."

Siegel stared at him, impressed with his thoroughness.

"So you're saying you've found us another place? One where the cops won't come looking for us?"

"It is all arranged. We will stay with someone I know I can trust absolutely."

"You can't *know* you can trust *anyone* like that. Not — well, in our line of business, anyway."

"Perhaps so, but sometimes trust is all we have. You and I must trust one another as we must trust Don Mancini. For what it is worth I trust the people where we are going more than I trust you or Meyer or Frank. Do you trust Esta?"

"What kind of a question is that? She's my wife. But I don't tell her about my business. I keep her and my girls out of all that stuff."

"Exactly. And so do I keep business away from people I trust. When I tell you that I *know* we will be safe where we are going it is precisely *because* we are staying among those who are — not of our organization."

"Okay, Luigi, I got that. We're going to be staying with civilians. But come on, you can tell me when, where and who. Christ, we're supposed to be a team!"

"Yes, we're a team. And I know back in America you call the shots and I'm just a poor foot soldier. But on this one mission — with everything that's at stake — Meyer and Frank have agreed that I have to be the one in charge, the general if you like. I'll take you where we're going and you'll see soon enough why it's ideal and why I don't want to tell you a damn thing till the time comes."

"The hell with that! I got just as much chance of getting killed as you have but you won't tell me anything.

Fine, forget it; I'll go into Rome on my own and finish the job!"

"In your dreams. You don't know the city like I do, you can't speak the language, I can beat you at rifle shooting with my left hand and you're a loose cannon waiting to explode. At least I've got everything set up while I've been out. What have you been doing while I've been away?"

"Well, I haven't exactly been busy like you," he said with a smug smile of satisfaction. "I fucked a broad — some tart Don Mancini sent round."

For a moment Carmona was tempted to hit him.

"For Christ's sake, can't you keep your dick in your pants? Damn fool, you might jeopardize our whole mission!"

"What, you expect me to live like a monk? I've been climbing the walls with boredom and so what if I screw a broad? She's only a two-bit whore anyway. She knows nothing."

"Benny, this cop is arresting Mafiosi. The girl may be only a small part of the jigsaw but she can link you and me to Don Mancini. I don't care how many women you have when this mission's over but till then you do exactly what I tell you. So don't carry on like an idiot. No arguments."

Siegel stood up and towered over his partner.

"I'm sick of you telling me what to do. You can't talk to me this way. Back home I call the shots and I give the orders! And nobody dares to call me a fool!"

"You're not back home now. You're in a foreign country and you can't do things on your own here. When

Don Mancini gets back I'll tell him we're moving to a place I found myself. He'll give us the equipment we need to do the job and we'll be on our way."

"Yeah, yeah, keep me in the dark like always. You seriously think I'm some kind of snitch?"

"Go to hell! I've had enough of your attitude. I always knew there'd be a downside with you tagging along but I hadn't realized just how much of a liability you'd turn out to be."

"Screw you! I've had it up to here with *your* goddamn attitude!"

He pushed the older man and Carmona swung a punch in return that missed by inches. Suddenly the two of them were squaring up to each other and a fight broke out. Punches were thrown and insults traded and the noise brought Don Mancini's two henchmen rushing in.

"Hey, what are you doing?" asked Moretti.

"Butt out of it!" Siegel yelled.

As he was speaking Carmona landed a punch and Siegel grabbed his gun and pointed it at him. Carmona glared at him coldly.

"Yeah, that's real smart. Go right ahead and shoot me. If you got the balls. That'd be the end of our mission right there and then!"

As Siegel hesitated Carmona moved quickly. A left jab made him stagger and Carmona threw in an uppercut that landed squarely on the point of his chin. Siegel toppled on to the floor and into unconsciousness. As the two minders stared at Carmona, uncertain how to react to the new situation, he switched to Italian.

"He's gone a bit crazy but he'll be all right later. No need to worry."

Moretti was clearly shaken by the fight and stared at Carmona in a state of shock.

"What's his problem?"

"In America he is a big *capo*. Here he is only a soldier who must take orders from me. And he does not like it."

"I understand."

Carmona cursed his bad luck in being saddled with such a volatile and difficult partner. *I'm almost tempted to leave him here to be arrested.* Knowing he could never do that, he turned to Moretti.

"How long will it be before the Don arrives?"

"Not long now. What are you going to tell him about this?"

Carmona considered his options for a moment.

"We'll say he got drunk. As soon as the Don arrives I need to ask him to get us out of here. If we could arrange to drop me and Benny somewhere in central Rome we can make our own way from there. Best nobody knows where we're staying. That way Bellini's got nothing to go on."

The door opened and everyone was instantly alert. Mancini came in with two toolboxes and everyone relaxed when they saw him. He looked at Carmona as he saw Siegel sprawled out on the sofa.

"Is he drunk?"

"Don't worry, Don Mancini, he will be sober tomorrow. You have the guns and the other stuff we need?"

"It's all there in the toolbox."

Carmona raised the question of their immediate evacuation from the safe house.

"Bellini has arrested some of your people today and they may come here at any time. We need to leave and go into central Rome. If you could drop us there I have already made other arrangements for our stay in the city."

"I already know about Bellini's raid today. He has caught only small fish in his net but you're right, we must be careful. If you say you have found a place of safety then we will drop you wherever you wish to go and let you find your own way there. Good luck with the job."

The two men hugged each other.

"We will not forget all your kindness to us and you can rest assured that Don Costello will hear of your great services and reward you handsomely for all the help you have given us."

Mancini smiled and pointed to the toolboxes.

"Everything you need is in there. All we have to do now is finalize your escape route. Here is the plan I have drawn up."

Carmona and Mancini went through the proposals in great detail. He made certain that every aspect of the escape route was firmly committed to his memory. Now was the time to make preparations for their departure. Carmona destroyed all evidence they had been there and wiped down all surfaces to eradicate any trace of fingerprints. The clothes and rifles were packed securely and then the two henchmen lifted the unconscious Siegel up and carried him through the back door to the waiting car He slumped in the back seat and they covered him up with a blanket.

Exiting the garage as soundlessly as possible they drove the car slowly along the road and headed for the Piazza Venezia. They drove through quiet, almost deserted roads until they arrived in the centre of Rome. It was a few hours after midnight when they reached it following a twenty-minute drive. The streets were empty apart for a few transitory drunks, the road-sweepers were busy cleaning the streets with their long brooms and colonies of stray cats were rifling the dustbins of the city in search of discarded items of food. In the back seat of the car a groaning noise began to be heard as Siegel slowly regained consciousness.

They took Siegel out of the car and laid him on a bench in the square. Carmona shook hands with the henchmen and said his farewells. He watched them disappear before he sat down and waited for his comrade to come round. He twitched slightly as consciousness began to return while he watched him with a mixture of exasperation and grudging respect for his stubborn refusal to back down.

"You'll be fine now."

Siegel stirred and sat up on the bench. He glared at Carmona with a cold fury in his eyes, trying to remember what happened.

"Don't ever do that again. Next time I'll fucking kill you!"

"Let's hope there isn't a next time. We need to focus on the job ahead. Pretty soon we'll be picked up by my contact and taken to a place of safety."

He heard the sound of an engine and hoped it was Fredo's truck. As it approached he hailed it and his uncle parked up on the opposite side of the road. Carmona waved across to him and the driver responded with a wave of his own. Leaving Siegel on the bench he wandered across to the vehicle and gazed inside the cab.

"Thank God it's you, Uncle Fredo."

"Who else were you expecting?"

"I wasn't sure. We'd better get in quick."

Fredo signalled his agreement and Carmona put the toolboxes in the pick-up before he covered it with some tarpaulin. Turning to Siegel he motioned to him to follow.

"This is my uncle Fredo. This is Benny."

Siegel grunted non-committally. He was still too angry to talk and Fredo was already under enough stress. Carmona could only hope he'd calm down by the time they arrived at his uncle's place.

The rest of the journey passed in silence. Within ten minutes the truck pulled up at Fredo's house in Trastavere. He leapt out and opened the wooden doors to his garage. Siegel had woken up at last and though still drowsy was at least able to walk but Carmona pulled him along to make sure that he came with them. After the garage doors were locked they walked up the narrow internal staircase until they arrived inside Fredo's apartment.

"Well," Fredo said, "you'd better tell me exactly what's going on here and what happens next."

Carmona made sure that the toolboxes were securely stowed away before answering.

"Hard to know where to start," he said. "You heard of Benny Siegel?"

"Should I have done?"

"Maybe it's better you don't know. Anyway you're looking at him right now. He's my partner in this — enterprise. And don't worry, we're only staying with you a couple of nights. Then it's time for us to leave and do the job."

Fredo's hands shook slightly as he glanced at his nephew.

"Please be careful. What you propose to do is very dangerous."

"Let us hope God is with us and will protect us as he did Moses."

Siegel began looking around Fredo's apartment with a feeling of utter disbelief. It had only two rooms and both the water supply and toilet were outside the home and shared with other tenants. The kitchen consisted of a cupboard standing next to a gas hob with two rings in a corner of the living room. There was no sink and only enamel bowls, buckets and jugs of water served for the household ablutions. A small balcony overlooked the narrow street.

The little furniture Fredo possessed consisted of two threadbare armchairs, a kitchen table and four rickety kitchen chairs. On hand-built shelves he saw the menorah displayed together with a few books and some glass ornaments.

The apartment was clean but untidy with newspapers and paper bags littering the floor. Siegel stared, reflecting that the last time he saw poverty like this was as a child growing up on the East Side of New York. Even that was better than this. He felt sorry for him and could see he'd obviously worked hard all of his life but had nothing to show for it.

The realization of Fredo's desperate poverty made him feel humble and overcame his anger at Carmona's high-handed behaviour.

"What part of the city am I in?"

"You are in the safest possible part of Rome."

"What the hell does that mean?"

"Trastavere. It's the Jewish part of the city."

"I didn't know there was one."

"My uncle Fredo has kindly agreed to put us up for a couple of days. So pull yourself together and show some respect."

Siegel gave him a fixed stare, still unable to forgive him for defeating him.

"Does he know why we're in Rome?"

"Yes, he does. He knows we're working for the U.S. government and what our mission here is."

Siegel digested the new cover story Carmona had just sprung upon him. *I hadn't thought of that. Yes, maybe he is a Fed. Am I being set up as the fall guy for a U.S. government hit? I can't trust him at all. From now on I'm going to watch everything he says and does.*

"What happens now?"

Carmona knew that he had taken a tremendous risk by telling him the story he'd already given his uncle. *It's a hell of a gamble and he'll think I'm trying to use him as cover and I'm going to throw him to the wolves when I kill Hitler. But I couldn't tell my uncle that we're supposed to be a pair of criminals working for the Mafia. I can only hope he has the sense to understand and at least to keep quiet and not give away his true identity. Maybe the fact that he didn't react when I said that means that he understands. Either way, we'll both have to be careful of each other.*

"After today I'm not so sure I wouldn't be better off doing the job on my own. This place is ideal for us to stay because the police won't think of coming here to search for us and Mancini doesn't know about it either. So we have total security here. Tomorrow morning we'll go to the apartment block I found. One of them is perfect for what we need. Now I think we should get some sleep. The next two days are going to be the roughest and most dangerous of our lives. So let's get ready for a long day tomorrow."

14

Lieutenant Marco Bellini was a rising star in the Rome police force. An ambitious man, he had risen to the rank of Lieutenant in a short time and with a young wife and two young children to support, he worked tirelessly.

He thought that today would be just another day in the office. Glancing briefly at the paperwork on the arrest sheets he sat at his desk and prepared to interview the suspects they had arrested the previous day at the garment factory. There was no reason to suspect anything out of the ordinary; the usual round-up of small-time Mafia suspects who would be locked up for a short time and then return to their previous activities.

As he looked at the headlines on the morning paper his normally impassive face frowned slightly. The news was full of the imminent arrival in Italy of the German Chancellor for a state visit. He was due in two days' time and the resources of the police would be stretched to breaking point providing even tighter security.

That bastard Hitler, Bellini thought. He's a dangerous maniac and Mussolini is vain enough to fall for his flattery. All Hitler wants is to drag my country into a war on his side.

To take his mind off the news he put down the paper and looked once again at the arrest sheets in front of him. The first name on the list was a familiar adversary. Bellini had arrested him three times in the last five years but the man continued his Mafia activities in spite of the short jail terms he had already served. Picking up the phone, he gave his instructions to the desk sergeant.

"Send him in," he said.

Bellini briefly interviewed the man and charged him before sending him back to his cell. The next three suspects were equally routine. *All petty criminals, he thought sourly, little fish that he'd lock up for a few months and then would be free to resume their criminal activities once more.*

The next interview went rather differently. A young man swaggered into the room and sat down with a boastful expression on his face.

"Franco Varese. This is the first time we've met. A new kid on the block, I suppose."

"Don't call me a kid. I'm twenty-four and that makes me a man!"

The arrogance in the man's voice surprised Bellini. He looked up from his paperwork and gazed intently at his latest suspect. Bellini observed at once that he was dressed in the latest fashion, held himself with obvious self-assurance and seemed indifferent to the fact that he had just been arrested.

"Are you fond of our prisons? Because that is exactly where you will be spending the next few months."

"Yeah, Mr Big Cop, locking up us little guys when all we're trying to do is earn a living. We're businessmen, entrepreneurs. You ought to be proud of us instead of locking us up."

Bellini rarely smiled but it was with some difficulty that he prevented himself from doing so now.

"Really? You're a businessman? In that case I'm sure that you know that businesses have to operate within the law. And the last time I checked your line of business was against the law."

"Law! Mussolini makes the law. We got on fine with the law before he came along!"

Bellini had to admit that the Mafia hoodlum had a point. Before Mussolini had become his country's leader no Italian Prime Minister had even attempted to root out the scourge of the Mafia, preferring to strike corrupt bargains with them and leave them unmolested.

"I take it you are not an admirer of Il Duce. Of course that kind of talk is outright sedition. Perhaps even treason. Such a crime would earn you some years in prison rather than a few months."

At those words Varese's blustering self-confidence seemed to melt away. He stared at the officer for a moment nervously before speaking again.

"What if we could make a deal?"

"A deal? You can't bribe me!"

"No, not that kind of a deal. What if I was to — tell you something?"

"What, information in return for leniency? I doubt very much if a low-grade Mafiosi like you could possibly know anything of interest to me."

Ignoring the insult, Varese pressed on with his attempted plea-bargain.

"You'll want to hear *this* piece of news."

"Very well. What is this news that you consider so important that it would make me ready to do a deal with you?"

"Two rifles have gone missing. The latest thing — the real deal, the high-powered Karabiner 98 Kurz sniper rifle. And you can guess who they're going to be aimed at soon enough!"

"Perhaps you should enlighten me. Are you implying that you know about an assassination plan?"

Varese hesitated before he finally answered that question.

"Not exactly. But I know two sniper rifles went missing from the barracks and they're going to be used in a hit any day soon."

"And why should I believe you? Or imagine that even if what you said is true that the guns are not simply going to be used in another of your Mafia wars?"

Varese was sweating but he had gone too far to back out now.

"Let's say you check with the army. You'll find the paperwork's in order but if you ask them to do a manual count they'll find there's two guns missing. And who do you think is going to be making a lot of public appearances for the best part of a week? With Hitler's state visit he'll be on display a lot."

Bellini was alert and interested now. He started to believe the young thug in front of him.

"Are you saying there's a plot to assassinate Il Duce?"

"I don't actually *know* that but that would be my guess. I mean, why get two high-powered sniper rifles for an ordinary hit? We could kill our own people easily enough with hand guns."

Bellini became thoughtful at those words. It seemed unlikely that if the man was telling the truth the rifles would have been stolen for any purpose other than to assassinate Mussolini.

"I will make some enquiries. But if you have been wasting my time you'll regret it."

Once Varese was back in his cell Bellini rang the army barracks in Rome.

"This is Lieutenant Marco Bellini of the Carabinieri," he said. "I want you to check out a possible theft at the barracks. We've had a report that two Karabiner 98 Kurz sniper rifles have been stolen from the base. Check the records but also get the ordnance officer to do a manual count of the weapons. Thank you. I'll wait to hear back from you."

Bellini went methodically through the pile of paperwork on his desk. He knew that somewhere within the morass of data he would find a name, a fact or something that would help him discover the identity of the assassins. Two rifles had been stolen so there must be a team of killers. In some ways that made his task easier; in other ways it made it harder to track them down.

When his contact at the barracks rang back to confirm the theft of the rifles Bellini immediately telephoned his superior officer. Captain Luca Solanio understood at once the significance of the theft of two such high-powered weapons. He agreed with Bellini that they were more likely to be used in an assassination rather than a simple Mafia killing. He also regarded Varese's confession as supporting the idea that the target of such an attack would almost certainly be Mussolini. Solanio promised to speak to the Chief of Police and then issue further instructions. He would ask the Chief to try and persuade Mussolini to cancel or at least scale-down some of his forthcoming public appearances during Hitler's state visit.

In his office Bellini pondered the future. Much as he disliked Mussolini he knew that it was his job to protect him and the idea that he might be assassinated because of an act of negligence or a casual oversight on his part filled him with horror. Hitler and Mussolini would be making numerous public appearances and it was obvious that Il Duce would be much more vulnerable than usual. The visit was due to begin in two days' time and that gave him hardly any time to make proper investigations. There were so many people who would be willing to assassinate Mussolini that it would be a nightmare eliminating all the possible killers.

Wiping the sweat from his brow with a silk handkerchief he ordered Varese to be brought before him once more.

When Varese entered the room Bellini resumed his interrogation.

"Who is your Don?"

Varese did not answer. He knew that the young thug would not be easy to break down but was determined to make him talk.

"You do realize that conspiracy to murder Il Duce will mean a death sentence, don't you? Unless you tell me the truth you will be charged with treason and you will certainly be executed for it."

Varese went pale when he heard those words. He had not expected that response and suddenly his bargaining chip looked more like a deadly weapon aimed at his own head.

"But I know nothing about such things," he said, trembling at the prospect that suddenly unfolded before him. "I swear to you I know nothing. All I did was overhear a conversation."

Bellini felt a sense of exultation as he prepared to close the trap.

"So you say. Perhaps if you told me the truth I could help you but unless you give me the names of your Don and the men you heard talking I can do nothing."

Varese gazed around the room helplessly, torn between his fear of betraying the oath of silence and the fear of being executed if he upheld it. Realizing the conflict within the mind of his prisoner Bellini returned him to his cell to consider his position. He was confident now that Varese would soon crack and reveal the names he needed.

As Bellini waited for his prisoner to break under the pressure Captain Solanio rang him. He was not surprised to hear that the assassination plot had now been given the highest possible priority.

"We will advertise in the newspapers and on the radio offering a reward for anyone who provides information leading to the capture of these two criminals alive or dead. In the meantime I will send someone to meet you. He's the most likely person to be able to identify the two Mafiosi and lead us to them. It is imperative that we stop these assassins before they succeed in killing Il Duce. You are in full daily charge of the investigation, Marco. I expect results and you must liaise with me on a regular basis. Is that understood?"

"Of course, Captain. Who is this man that I must meet? And how soon will it be before I speak with him?"

"It is a man whose name will be familiar to you. I am sending Vito Genovese to meet you."

Bellini was so astonished at the name of the man he was due not simply to meet but also to work with that he almost questioned his superior officer before biting back the angry retort that lingered briefly upon his lips. Instead he controlled his temper and waited for further instructions.

"I gather you know the man."

"I know of him, sir."

"Then you also know that he may well be the one man capable of providing us with the information we need. Genovese will arrive tomorrow morning. The two of you will share whatever information you have. Is that understood?"

"Perfectly, sir."

As he put down the phone Bellini cursed loudly. He was offended by the idea of working with a Mafia Don like Genovese and furious at being ordered to share his own information with a vicious thug.

Morning came to Rome and Bellini waited in his office for the arrival of his visitor. As he sat at his desk gazing for the third time that day at the brief case notes he had been able to assemble a knock came at the door.

"Lieutenant, Signor Genovese to see you."

"Show him in."

The door opened and Bellini gazed up from his desk as the man entered. He strutted inside the office and his air of arrogance offended Bellini almost as much as his criminality. He was above the law and knew it. On his return to Italy he had presented Mussolini with a large

102

amount of money in return for being allowed to conduct his criminal activities without interference from the authorities. Some accounts said it was half a million dollars, others said a million or even more. Whatever the sum it had been sufficient to give him protection from the law.

Much as he hated and despised the man Bellini knew that he was untouchable. Head of the Mafia in Italy and yet he and his followers were completely exempt from the crackdown that Mussolini had ordered against the other criminal gangs.

"Sit down," he said, his voice anything but friendly. "My captain has ordered me to work with you on a delicate matter that concerns us both."

The Mafia Don insolently gave the grimace that passed for a smile with him. The right part of his mouth seemed higher than the left when he smiled and the effect was in marked contrast to the genial looking eyes that almost beamed out from behind the large square framed glasses.

Bellini watched his visitor sit down slowly in the chair and noted the expensive but baggy light grey double-breasted suit, the striped crimson tie and the white handkerchief protruding from his right breast pocket. His receding hair, large ears and prominent nose added to the effect of subtle menace disguised behind the apparently benevolent expression on his face.

"You can't touch me," said Genovese in a voice full of quiet menace. "All you can do is arrest a few minor players. I'm beyond your law and you'll never get your hands on me."

Bellini ignored the studied insult. Knowing that he had no choice but to work with this vicious thug he attempted to steer the interview towards finding the answers to at least some of his questions. It had been bad enough when Genovese was only a name but now that he had actually met the man his dislike for him was intense. How he could be expected to work with this gangster was beyond him. All he knew was that those were his orders and so, reluctantly, he obeyed.

"Well, Signor Genovese, perhaps you can help me. We both know that there is a plot to assassinate Il Duce by certain elements of a criminal society. You are familiar with the name Frank Costello?"

Genovese studied the lieutenant intently before replying.

"I know the name, yes."

"And have you met him?"

"I used to know him a little in America."

Bellini was well aware of the fact that both Genovese and Costello had worked together on many criminal enterprises including murder and were now bitter enemies. Genovese had been angling to take over as head of the Syndicate but instead had been forced into exile in Italy while Costello had taken over Mafia operations in America. The two men hated each other and Bellini hoped that this mutual enmity might help him track down the assassins. Greed of course was an additional spur and he was sure that Genovese would try to claim the reward money for himself.

"Does Costello have influence among some criminal gangs in Italy?"

"Yes, he does."

"So do you of course," said Bellini smoothly. "And the feud between your organization and Costello's means that for entirely different reasons we are on the same side in this case. I will be frank with you, Signor Genovese. I want the two assassins captured or killed *before* they have a chance to attempt to kill Il Duce. There is a substantial reward for anyone who provides information leading to that outcome so co-cooperating with me against a mutual adversary would be doubly beneficial to you."

"How much? How big is this reward of yours?"

"A quarter of a million dollars."

The eyes of the mobster did not move but he twitched slightly as he took in the news. It would be doubly pleasurable to foil Costello's plan and be handsomely rewarded for doing so.

"That's a lot of money."

"It certainly is to an honest man, Are you willing to help me find these killers?"

Genovese gave the same kind of predatory smile that legend has is seen on the face of the tiger as he fastens his eyes upon his prey.

"As a patriotic Italian how could I not wish to protect Il Duce?"

Bellini ignored the returned sarcasm from Genovese and tried to find answers to some of his most pressing questions.

"Would any Italian Don carry out such a project on his own authority?"

Genovese shook his head decisively.

"No, definitely not. None of them would have the balls or the capability. Except for me, of course. But as I have an excellent relationship with Il Duce that is out of the question. No, the order must have come from America. That means Frank Costello. He would have to be the one who authorised such a project."

"And presumably he has people here in Italy ready to follow his commands?"

"Unfortunately he does."

Bellini was becoming increasingly tired of the game he was being forced to play with the Mafia boss.

"Would he use local people to attempt the killing?"

Genovese stared at the police office briefly and considered his answer.

"Probably. Of course he has numerous soldiers under his control but they would almost all use revolvers. To steal two rifles argues an assassination by stealth and requires the services of trained marksmen. We are talking people who for example are or were in the army and probably expert snipers."

"How many men served in the war? Or since trained in the army? We must be looking at tens of thousands of possible snipers!"

"Yes, that's true. But how many of them are in your files? I know you keep dossiers on organizations. Perhaps a study of them might help you narrow the field down."

"Perhaps," said Bellini, almost as infuriated by the man's arrogance as by his utter immunity to legal sanctions. "Do you know a man called Varese?" he asked. "Franco Varese?"

Genovese denied any knowledge of the name and Bellini felt that the man probably was unknown to the Mafia boss.

"No matter. Ask your people to look for anyone they feel might be suspicious. As you know they will be well recompensed. We will announce the fact that we suspect a plot to assassinate Il Duce and that a reward is on offer. Hopefully that will make them keenly observant."

"I'm sure it will."

As soon as his unwelcome visitor had left the office Bellini got up and walked about the room. He felt an urgent desire to get out and breathe fresh air again. Somehow the presence of Genovese in his office had polluted his work-space and he felt unable to function without first putting some distance between himself and Genovese. He was about to leave and try to clear his head when the phone rang.

"Marco? Captain Solanio. We have discussed matters with Il Duce but he refuses absolutely to change his plans. We will have to protect him but in the meantime you must round up every Mafia member you can. Raid homes, restaurants, everywhere."

"Consider it done."

Bellini drew up a series of orders to search and detain "all those suspected of involvement with criminal gangs." Unofficially he realized that Genovese's people would have to be excluded from the crackdown but consoled himself with the thought that it might not be easy to distinguish between his men and Costello's particularly in the initial stages of arrest.

The rest of the day saw a flurry of frantic activity as Bellini's men raided homes and businesses and arrested hundreds of suspects.

As they returned to Rome Bellini's thoughts were turning already to the following day when the news of the assassination plot and the reward would be broadcast on the radio and carried as front-page news in the press. He doubted that he would get much sleep in the near future and decided to interview as many of the new batch of suspects as possible.

Bellini focused his eyes through the office window onto the streets below. The rain beat down upon the streets of the eternal city, lashing the modern apartment blocks and ancient monuments with equal ferocity. *Somewhere in the heart of this city the two assassins are waiting. And I only have two days to stop them!*

15

While Carmona and Siegel took refuge in Trastavere from the police and possible traitors among the Mafia, Bellini remained vigilant and determined to pursue his investigation to the bitter end. For the last couple of days it seemed that his whole life had been put on hold until the state visit was over and he longed to be able to return to more routine police work. He felt as if he had taken root in his office and his head was frantically processing names, dates and places as he tried to establish a link between suspects and identify possible vantage points from which the assassins might strike.

Varese remained his best line of enquiry. Bellini had no illusions about Genovese's motives and expected no serious co-operation from him. *All that lowlife wants is the money. He has no more loyalty to Mussolini than anyone else. I don't think he cares if the assassination succeeds or not. All he wants is to kill the assassins and claim the reward. And I've been ordered to work with him!*

His face flushed as he felt increasingly frustrated by the way in which political considerations were preventing him from conducting a proper enquiry. If Genovese did not have such close links with the Fascist Party he would cheerfully have arrested him and all his crew

He had barely seen his family since he first heard the news of the planned assassination. His wife and their two children had become used to his frequent absences from home but because of the present threat he had seen almost nothing of them.

Rousing himself from his desk he re-interviewed Varese.

"This is your last chance. Either you co-operate fully or I'll charge you with conspiracy to murder and high treason. You know what will happen if you're charged with those crimes, don't you? Your only hope is to tell me everything you know."

The inner struggle was etched on Varese's face like a plate treated with acid. Bellini sensed that now was the time to reel in his fish.

"Well, Franco," he said, switching to the prisoner's first name," I hope you've given a lot of thought to your position. If you can lead me to the assassins I'll see to it that nothing bad happens to you. But if you don't help me I can't help you. I'm not interested in you; all I want is to stop the assassins."

Varese gazed at the lieutenant with a thoroughly beaten look in his eyes. He knew the game was up but was also terrified of betraying the code of silence.

"I honestly don't know who they are. I overheard a conversation between two people I know, that's all."

Bellini realized that Varese probably knew very little but he was determined to extract every ounce of information from his suspect. He called for a chair to be brought in and gestured to Varese to sit down.

"Give me their names."

Varese looked up at the ceiling, desperate for a way out. Whatever he did might lead to serious trouble or even death.

"All I heard was two men discussing the theft of the rifles."

"And what exactly did they say?"

"They said that two Karabiner 98 Kurz rifles had been stolen from a barracks. Then they moved out of earshot."

"I see. And how do you know these people?"

"Sometimes we've done jobs together. Not often — about three times in all."

Bellini knew that although Varese was a low-level Mafiosi even the smallest detail might be crucial in terms of tracking down the assassins. He pursued his task of finding the evidence with the same degree of determination he imagined the assassins must have.

"Do you and the other two men have the same Don?"

"No."

"Who is your Don, Franco?"

Varese hesitated even longer. Bellini thought all his good work was about to go to waste. With a trembling voice he finally answered.

"Don Guardini."

Bellini leaned back in his chair and prepared to move in for the kill.

"And do you know which Don the other two — work for?"

"Yes."

To Bellini's surprise he seemed far less nervous about revealing the name of their Don than his own.

"They work for Don Mancini."

Bellini now had enough information to begin preliminary enquiries but needed authorization from his superior officer before he could proceed further. He had no doubt it would be forthcoming but the notoriously slow wheels of Italian bureaucracy moved even slower under fascism than previously.

"Go back to your cell for a while, Franco. I'll check out your information and we'll talk again later."

First he summoned a records clerk to check police files for any information on Guardini and Mancini. Before long two manila folders were brought to his desk. He worked through them methodically and noted that both men had been arrested several times but neither had ever been convicted. Knowing the extreme reluctance of witnesses to testify against Mafiosi he was not surprised but at least he now had names, faces and a list of places to search.

Picking up the phone he called Captain Solanio and explained the position to him. Solanio immediately authorized him to put out arrest warrants for both men and to search any properties connected with them. Gathering a squad of police officers together Bellini left his office at last and took charge of operations.

Teams of carabinieri were despatched to a number of addresses in Rome and the surrounding areas. Bellini went with three men to check on Mancini's safe-house. He was unaware that nobody lived there and the premises were only used for illegal business.

The sky above them was dark with heavy clouds and the rain pounded the squad car relentlessly throughout their drive. As they stepped out of the vehicle the wind and rain continued to assail them as they made their way towards the bungalow.

"Better draw your guns. Mancini may not come quietly."

The four men approached cautiously with their pistols drawn and stayed alert for the slightest sound or movement.

"Police! Come out with your hands up!".

No answer came and he decided to move towards the property.

"Proceed with extreme caution. They may be in hiding or they may have already gone but take no chances."

Two officers went round the back while one accompanied Bellini to the front door. He knocked hard but received no answer. There was no sound of any kind to indicate the presence of inhabitants and reluctantly he gave the order to force an entry.

As the front door yielded to pressure he stood in the doorway brandishing his gun. The two men entered and cautiously moved around the house. There was no one inside and after a few minutes he summoned the other two officers to join him in a search.

They collected as much material as they could and took it back to the station for analysis. The place had been wiped clean of fingerprints. There was no sign of Mancini or any of his minions and nothing they had found held any clues to the identity or whereabouts of the assassins. All he could do was hope that some of the other leads would bring results.

On his return to his office he gave immediate orders for the main railway station in Rome to be searched with minute precision. This was where Hitler was scheduled to meet with the king of Italy and Mussolini and this would be the first obvious opportunity for an assassin to strike. For hours the police scoured the station until they were satisfied that it was as secure as possible. Bellini went to sleep but his rest was troubled. The thought of the imminent danger to his country's leader was uppermost in his mind.

16

There were no spare beds in Fredo's apartment and it was clear that neither of his guests would enjoy a comfortable night's sleep. His sad eyes wandered around his home as he reflected upon how little he could offer his guests from America. *Here is my nephew Luigi, a man of substance and property, visiting his old uncle and yet I cannot even offer him a proper home.*

He began by offering his own bed but both Carmona and Siegel declined the offer. It was hard for him to fall asleep that night but he knew that he must. He knew that the approach of morning would bring him no comfort but simply represent the drawing nearer of impending danger. When Hitler paraded before the massed ranks of people in Rome Luigi and Benny would either shoot and hopefully kill him or be killed themselves.

They slept on the shabby armchairs in a sitting position with nothing but some faded overcoats to serve as bedding. The fastidious Siegel suffered more than his companion. Carmona had spent many days in cold, damp, insanitary and dangerous conditions while in the Italian army and had the knack of falling asleep instantly and awakening to full alertness with equal rapidity.

When the rays of the sun began to pierce the veil of darkness in the sky above them Fredo rose from his troubled sleep. He realized there was not enough food in the house and that he needed to go to the shops. As the two men woke at his approach he apologized for disturbing them and told them that he had to be seen or his neighbours would think that something was wrong.

"Especially at my age."

"Just make sure you don't mention anything about us."

Fredo looked at him with an injured expression in his eyes.

"Do you seriously think I would put you in danger? I will be the soul of discretion, I swear it."

Siegel and Carmona practised repeatedly assembling and loading their rifles and going over the plans. They were growing increasingly confident that the scheme might actually work. Their high spirits were dashed abruptly when Fredo returned with downcast eyes. In spite of repeated questions his uncle appeared quite unable to speak and was trembling with obvious agitation. Finally he threw down the newspaper and Carmona picked it up.

When he read the headline he knew at once what was wrong. The front page of the paper screamed the unwelcome news at him

TWO ASSASSINS PLOT TO KILL IL DUCE. LARGE REWARD FOR INFORMATION LEADING TO THEIR DISCOVERY.

Turning to Siegel, he told him the bad news.

"How the hell do they know?"

"I'll kill the fucking bastards who ratted us out!"

"Keep your voice down and stay calm.".

"What kind of lousy vermin would betray us for money? Who was it? Mancini? I bet it's that Moretti! I never trusted him from the moment I met him."

"We don't know who it was. It might even be that whore you fucked!"

"I didn't tell her anything. She doesn't even know who I am. It can't be her."

"Maybe this place is being staked out by the cops."

Going up to the window Siegel peered out through a gap in the curtains and looked outside.

"Can't see any cops, but maybe we should call the whole thing off."

Sweat was pouring from Siegel's brow as he paced up and down the room.

"Why are you so quiet, Luigi?"

"Shut up and sit down. I'm trying to figure out the situation."

Biting his lip Siegel sat down and waited. Carmona realized that this meant that their task would be even harder but he knew that panic was not the right way to react.

"It's obvious they don't know who we are or where we are. If they did we'd have been rounded up or killed already. And of course they think we're after a different target. So if we stick to our plan and stay vigilant we can still pull it off."

Then he went across to his uncle and handed him a glass of brandy. Fredo took it with a trembling hand and swallowed it quickly. He began to choke and Carmona led him into the kitchen.

"I'll cook some food," said Fredo. "It will help take my mind off things."

Lunch was a more subdued affair with the shock news making them quieter than usual. Fredo made Carmona's favourite meal, artichokes cooked in the Jewish way. The three of them sat glumly staring at the plates in front of them with the constant sound of the wireless in the background. As they mopped up the olive oil and garlic with their bread Carmona broke the silence at last.

"We must have the strength of our convictions. We must remember why we came here — to kill Hitler. Now is not the time to panic or lose sight of our goal. We must hold our nerve and if we do, we can and will succeed."

Siegel looked up from the plate and stared at him.

"Of course we can. You and me are primed and ready for action. But who can we trust now? We don't know who's on our side and who might turn us in for the reward money."

They sat in silence for a while, digesting the new situation.

"Uncle Fredo, we'll be gone tomorrow. Drop us off with our tools near the apartment block and we'll make our own way there. You drive off and forget about us for a while. We've got a big day tomorrow."

"Got any wine? Let's celebrate early!"

Fredo went into the kitchen and returned with two bottles of red wine.

"I think we all need a drink," he said.

As they savored the wine Carmona spoke to his uncle.

"It's our last day with you. When I get back to America I'm sending you the money to come over to the States. I'll look after you from now on."

Fredo nodded gratefully and embraced his nephew.

"Yes, I would like that. Before you leave me tomorrow is there anything else you still need from me?"

"Yes, we need two pairs of gloves, two neckerchiefs, two chisels, adhesive for tiles and some rope."

Fredo stared at his nephew in astonishment, wondering why he needed such unusual items.

"We'll be getting into the apartment posing as tilers repairing the mezzanine floors."

"And the rope?"

Carmona did not reply and changed the subject.

"When we've finished our drink I think we should turn in."

The three men drank and retired to bed. They knew tomorrow morning would be the most difficult and challenging day of their lives.

17

Benny Siegel had been right to distrust Alberto Moretti. His instinct when he met him at the safe house was correct. He had no loyalty to anyone, not even his own Don. Moretti cared about no one but himself.

As he listened to the news bulletin, Moretti realized he knew who the two assassins were. He was utterly indifferent to the fate of Mussolini but the amount of money being offered was enough to let him live in luxury for the rest of his days.

It was unthinkable that he would go to the police and pass on the information to them. On the other hand Moretti knew that there were two rival Mafias within Italy. One, to which he and Mancini belonged, was totally opposed to fascism and actively repressed by Mussolini. The other, led by Genovese, collaborated actively with the regime and was left alone by the authorities.

Within Moretti's mind the germs of an idea formed. *I'll go to Genovese and tell him what I know. He'll reward me for the information.*

He knew it would not be simple to approach him. Being a member of Mancini's gang he would automatically be distrusted and might even be suspected of laying a trap for them. How could he contact them and gain their confidence?

Moretti knew that a café in Rome was frequented by Genovese's followers. He decided to visit it and arrange a meeting with the boss.

He took a bus to the Termini station where he walked a few blocks to an undesirable district. Standing outside the Cafe Coppella he stared through the window. Moretti recognized two of Genovese's men leaning on a marble counter.

The inside of the cafe was spartan with a couple of old tables and chairs that were used for card playing and serving Frascati wine. The other four customers were eating pork stuffed with herbs between thick hunks of rustic bread. He entered and walked up to the two henchmen. They recognized him at once and challenged him as soon as he came inside.

"What do you want?" said the older of the two men in a menacing tone of voice.

"To see Don Genovese."

The man who had challenged Moretti turned to his colleague.

"Frisk him."

The other man patted Moretti down and found nothing.

"He's clean."

"What do you want with the boss?"

"Look, I've got information he'll want to know. If you're not interested that's fine by me. But it seems a shame to miss out on what could be a very good deal for everyone."

"Wait here. I'll see what the boss has to say."

He disappeared into an adjoining room and spoke briefly before returning.

"Follow me."

The two henchmen ushered him into a side room where Genovese sat having his lunch. He saw two more bodyguards sitting there as the Mafia boss stuck his fork into a large plate of offal and chewed vigorously on the liver and hearts.

Genovese looked up enquiringly and motioned to him to speak.

"I am Alberto Moretti, Don Genovese. I have information for you that I think you'll be very interested to hear."

Genovese did not suspend his relentless eating as he glanced briefly at the interloper. He nodded and beckoned him forward with his finger.

"So you are Alberto Moretti," he said, wiping his mouth with a napkin as he stared at his unexpected visitor. "What is this information you want to tell me?"

His eyes fixed on him with a predatory menace as he awaited the reply.

"You know I work for Don Mancini." Rivulets of sweat flowed down Moretti's face as he tried to make the words come out the way he wanted them to sound. "As you know there is a plot to assassinate Mussolini and a large reward for any information leading to their death or capture. Well, I know who the killers are. I looked after them for a couple of days."

He had Genovese's full attention now and did not waste the opportunity.

"What's more, I will pick them up at a warehouse at 12 noon after the assassination of Mussolini."

"I see," said Genovese, studying his visitor carefully. "And do you have names for the two assassins?"

"One is an Italian called Luigi. He is much quieter than the other one. The second man is an American. He's called Benny."

Genovese's fork hovered in his hand in a state of suspended animation. He froze into immobility for a moment before putting it down quietly upon the plate.

"Give me a description of this Benny!"

Moretti was surprised at his reaction and could only assume he knew who the American was.

"Well, he's about 6 feet tall, athletic with short black hair and in his early thirties."

"Is he good looking with piercing blue eyes?"

"Yes, he is. He's also got a moustache."

Genovese banged on the table.

"I don't care about his moustache. I know why he's grown that!"

As he glared at Moretti almost as if it was his fault that he knew one of the gunmen he turned to his henchmen.

"It's Bugsy Siegel, that smart-assed gunman. He always likes to do a killing himself rather than simply arrange matters."

Moretti was stunned by Genovese's reaction to the news. Even he had heard of Bugsy Siegel and his reputation as a ruthless gangster with a string of killings to his name.

"I had no idea who he was, Don Genovese."

Genovese stabbed the meat on his plate.

"Never mind that. He's here now and we have to deal with him and his accomplice. Where were you supposed to meet him?"

Moretti gave him the location of the warehouse and the details were written down.

"You don't know where he went after he left you?"

"No, we dropped them off in central Rome and then drove away. I expect someone else must have picked them up."

Genovese began considering where the two assassins might have gone. It had to be in Rome but it could not be any of Mancini's Mafia hideouts. The police would have raided them by now and anyway Siegel would no longer trust them. Who else did he know in Rome?

He knew that on his previous visits to Italy Siegel had stayed at a villa on the outskirts of Rome with his lover. She was an Italian countess now but before her marriage had been an American actress in Hollywood. Would Siegel stay with her while he plotted his attempt on Mussolini?

He considered the idea briefly and then dismissed it as unlikely. The countess was too well known and Siegel would probably not want to expose his lover to the wrath of the fascists if he killed Mussolini. Even so he decided to order his people to check out the villa and put it under surveillance just in case he turned up there.

The other man was a mystery. All that he had was his first name and a description that could fit thousands of Italians. Luigi was hardly an uncommon Christian name and his physical appearance — medium build, short, early fifties — was hardly enough to identify him. Moretti did not know him so he must have come over from America with Siegel rather than being a local Mafia soldier. An Italian who had emigrated to America and returned to help carry out the assassination and almost certainly worked for Costello — there were too many people who could fit that particular bill.

Genovese gave up on the idea of tracking down Luigi. As an Italian who had probably not even lived in the country for some years there would be no trail to follow. He could have gone to ground anywhere in Rome probably with family members. Siegel must be lying low with him somewhere in the city and the chances of his reappearance before the assassination were slim.

Genovese dismissed the idea of finding the two assassins before they carried out the hit. His best chance was to wait until Siegel and Luigi turned up for their rendezvous at the warehouse. It did not matter to him one way or another if Mussolini was killed. His son-in-law Count Ciano would take over as leader and he was totally dependent on Genovese for his drug addiction. But the idea of killing Siegel certainly appealed to him. *I'll let him walk into a trap and gun him down. That would be a sweet revenge for the way he sided with Costello against me.*

"Well, Alberto, you've done me a service today. Of course I'll get my people to try and track them down but just in case we can't you'd better stay with us for the time being."

Moretti knew at once that it was a command and not a request. In spite of his increasing nervousness he had no choice but to agree.

"So if necessary you'll have to go with three of my soldiers to the warehouse to make the assignation with Siegel and Luigi. Then we'll kill them both."

Moretti agreed though he did not fancy the odds. He had seen enough of Siegel to know he was a borderline psychopath as well as a crack shot and Luigi was obviously a professional killer too. He was trapped now though and unable to go back now he had made the decision to contact Genovese and betray his own Don. Whichever way he looked at the situation he was in trouble.

"I understand."

Genovese did not even bother to reply but beckoned one of his henchmen across to the table.

"Take Alberto to a safe place. We'll need him to go with the hit squad to identify Siegel. Meanwhile I'll do some digging and see if I can pinpoint places in Rome where he might be hiding out."

Moretti was quickly ushered out of the restaurant through the kitchens and into a car parked round the back. He found himself in a small flat and one of the men from the restaurant remained behind. It was obvious that Genovese did not trust him and wanted to have him under lock and key until the time came for him to meet the two assassins at the warehouse.

18

Hitler had admired Mussolini ever since the Italian leader had made his famous March on Rome in 1922. That exploit led to the resignation of the Italian government and the king of Italy had appointed Mussolini as Prime Minister. The era of fascism began. Hitler was so inspired by Mussolini's rise to power that it was a major factor impelling him to carry out his own failed putsch in 1923.

He not only admired Mussolini personally but also regarded him as a natural ally. The large German population in South Tyrol had been part of Italy since the end of the Great War and many Nazis wanted them to become part of the Reich. Hitler disagreed and consistently refused to raise the issue.

With the prospect of war over the Sudeten Germans in Czechoslovakia, Hitler wanted to make sure that Italy would not side with Britain and France. At the least he wanted Italian neutrality and ideally military assistance in the event of a conflict.

The two nations had been jointly intervening in the Spanish Civil War. For two years Italian troops, ships and aircraft and some German soldiers and planes had been supporting Franco's rebellion. This military collaboration gave Hitler great encouragement about the prospects of Italian support against the Czechs.

Mussolini had his own territorial ambitions for Italy. He was already talking to the Fascist Grand Council about turning the Mediterranean into "an Italian lake" and had told them of his desire to expand into Albania, Yugoslavia, Greece and North Africa and eventually to "reclaim" the French Riviera from France. His navy was one of the strongest in the world and his Air Force was also one of the best. Italian aviation was close to developing jet aircraft and Mussolini felt confident that in the future he could create what was often referred to as "a new Roman Empire."

Goebbels and Himmler did not share Hitler's admiration for Mussolini. Both belonged to the socialist wing of the Nazi Party and Goebbels was a former Communist.

"I think Adolf is too easily by impressed by Mussolini," Goebbels said. "I don't look on Italian fascism as being the same as National Socialism. It's too capitalist for my liking."

"I feel the same. Mussolini has allowed the conservatives to dominate his agenda rather than pushing the true radicalism he began with."

"And, of course, as Alfred Rosenberg is always saying, it's racially confused and doesn't have the right attitude towards the Jews. Alfred thinks it's been too influenced by philo-Semitism rather than, like our movement, anti-Semitism."

"Of course in Adolf's eyes he is a great statesman and world leader. He made himself master of Italy ten years before we came to power in Germany. But in my opinion for all his pomp and strutting Mussolini is not like Adolf. He is a man of steel and vision while Mussolini is all dress suits stuffed with sawdust."

Hitler's own territorial ambitions lay mostly in Eastern Europe and Russia. He was content to allow the Italians to dominate the Mediterranean and North Africa. For him the South Tyrol was a price worth paying to have Mussolini as an ally if it came to war.

Now he was meeting Mussolini on a state visit to Italy. During the course of his stay he meant to cement the alliance between their countries and ensure that Italy would not stand against Germany as they had during the Great War.

The idea of a state visit to Italy excited nearly every senior Nazi. Hess, Himmler, Goebbels and Ribbentrop all insisted on accompanying Hitler and their wives also came along for the journey. Hitler invited his mistress, Eva Braun, to join him though not in an official capacity but under cover of being one of his secretaries.

Five hundred people accompanied him on the five trains that departed from Germany for Italy. A huge quantity of luggage filled the compartments and with the prospect of shopping in Italy many of the wives planned to add to its volume before returning home.

As the train crossed the border it halted at the Brenner Pass where Italian troops greeted them. There were huge floral displays and an array of banners welcoming them to Italy. A band played the national anthems of Germany and Italy while a man stepped forward and made the formal speech greeting the visitors at the station.

"I am the Duke of Pistoia," he said. "In the name of King Victor Emanuel I, welcome to Italy as our guests."

Both sides of the railway tracks were lined with soldiers forming a guard of honour. Every house they passed by as the train continued its journey was hung with banners and slogans proclaiming the deep friendship between the German and Italian people and praising Hitler.

***

Bellini glanced anxiously at his watch as he waited expectantly at the train station in Rome. For over an hour he and his men had been standing in position waiting for the arrival of Hitler. He scanned the surroundings with relentless vigour and watched for the slightest sign of any possible trouble but everything appeared normal.

The train pulled into the terminus at last. Mussolini had ordered the station to be built specially for the occasion and Bellini watched their arrival with nervous anticipation. As Hitler got out of the train he saw the familiar figure of the diminutive king of Italy stepping forward to greet him. The German Chancellor acknowledged the welcome but was privately furious that Mussolini had not come to greet him but had allowed the king to welcome him to Rome. The king's equerry led Hitler to the state carriage.

The vehicle had served the Italian monarchy for many years and in spite of its relative antiquity was an impressive sight. It glistened with the sheen created by the loving care of generations of craftsmen who maintained it on behalf of the monarchy. Four horses were positioned at the front, the finest stallions in the royal stables. They neighed as the two men who would share the carriage approached them.

Hitler glanced at the horse-drawn carriage with an air of total disdain upon his face. *This is the king of Italy and he expects us to travel in this, he thought angrily. Hasn't the House of Savoy ever heard of the motor car?*

Ignoring all protocol Hitler sat down in the carriage before the king. Victor Emanuel was offended but said nothing. The carriage prepared to depart and began its leisurely journey towards the royal palace.

The coach travelled the ancient road where in times gone past Roman Emperors had boasted to the people of their conquests in a triumphant procession. The fountains along the route were lit up in a dazzling light show and blazing torches and flashing searchlights illuminated every part of the way they travelled. Crowds lined the streets and applauded Hitler as he passed along the thoroughfares of Rome.

Hitler was startled for a moment as a troop of African cavalry appeared and rode straight at him in a regimental charge. With a faint smile Victor Emanuel assured his guest that it was simply an entertainment in his honour and that he was in no danger from the armed riders.

Hitler arrived at the Quirinale, the royal palace, in a bad temper. He had come to Italy with high hopes of concluding a formal military alliance and getting Mussolini to agree to his plans for the incorporation of Czechoslovakia within Germany yet already he felt that Mussolini had slighted him. He had spent almost the whole time since his arrival with the king and the dislike between the two men was clearly mutual. *These monarchies never do any good, he thought. If only Il Duce could rule Italy as I do Germany!*

Bellini heard the news that the king, Mussolini and Hitler had all arrived at their destinations safely. With considerable relief he decided to try and get some sleep. Tomorrow would be a long day with a number of possible danger areas. So far everything had gone smoothly and he could snatch some rest. *I'll be glad when this whole state visit is over,* he thought before turning in for the night.

19

While Genovese made his plans to remove Siegel and his associate, in another part of Rome the two assassins were beginning the final stage of their own preparations for murder. The heavy downpour of rain during the night had now ceased. The air was fresh and the streets looked cleaner.

Fredo had to take a diversion around the streets of Rome as the traffic control officers were now sealing off large areas of the city in preparation for the imminent arrival of Hitler. He dropped Siegel and Carmona off a few blocks away from the Via Florio, which was only a short walk from the apartment complex. The two men stepped out of the van and turned towards Fredo.

Siegel spoke first and with genuine affection thanked him for all he had done and to Fredo's embarrassment insisted upon pressing two hundred dollars into his hand.

Carmona waited a moment before hugging his uncle in a close and warm embrace and kissing him upon both cheeks.

"When this is over, Uncle Fredo, I'll send you the money and tickets for a ship out of this place. You can join me and start a new life in America."

As he parted Carmona also gave his uncle a hundred dollars in notes. Tears filled the eyes of both men as they took their farewells. Each one knew it might be the last time they saw each other alive.

"Take care, Luigi. Mind you don't miss!"

"We won't."

He turned away and began walking along the street in the direction of the apartment complex. As the two men checked their watches Siegel whispered to Carmona.

"It's ten in the morning. Only another 24 hours to go!"

"Yes, we'll be ready and waiting."

Rome was buzzing with activity as the finishing touches were made to the preparations for the many events planned to begin tomorrow. Shopkeepers decked out their premises in bunting and national flags. Street vendors made ready for what they hoped would be a prosperous day for them with the influx of visitors and even foreign tourists. The main thoroughfare heaved with people and as the assassins struggled forward they were forced to push their way through the teeming crowds. Neither the press of people nor the drizzle falling upon them from the sky above dampened their spirits or made them weaken in their determination to finish their mission.

"Here it is," said Carmona. "Now all we have to do is get inside!"

Dressed in their grey workmen's overalls which covered the suits underneath they placed their toolboxes on the step. No one would have guessed that inside those boxes were the two rifles they planned to use to kill Hitler.

Lighting up a cigarette Carmona and Siegel waited outside the apartment block. They knew eventually someone would either enter or leave and as soon as they did they were ready to take advantage. Within a few minutes the door opened from the inside and an elderly woman came out.

"Good morning, Signora," said Carmona in a cheerful voice. "Could you hold the door open for us while we take our tools inside?"

"What is your business here? You can't be too careful now with two maniacs on the loose!"

"I know what you mean. I only wish I knew who they were. The reward would let us retire and live a life of ease. But I'm afraid we're only builders from Pescaro and Co and they've sent us here to check the tiles on the mezzanine floors," he explained.

"Yes, there are quite a few loose and cracked tiles. I'm glad they're finally doing something about it."

She held the door open for them and the two men stepped inside. As soon as the door banged behind them they entered a cool, quiet vestibule and heaved a sigh of relief.

"Well, at least we're inside the building now. One step closer to the final goal! Now be quiet and pretend to work. We'll get the tiling tools out and slowly make our way up the stairs floor by floor."

The two men began taking the tiling tools from the box and pretending to examine the floor carefully. Inch by inch they made their way up the floors and climbed the stone staircase until they reached the third floor. Clinging on to the wrought iron balustrade they looked around them constantly and took in every aspect of the layout of the building.

After what seemed an eternity they found themselves standing outside the door of the apartment from which they planned to assassinate Hitler. They looked at each other and stood there waiting. They could hear the wireless in the background so they knew that someone was inside the flat. Siegel wanted to knock on the door but Carmona shook his head as he began to approach it.

"Not yet. We will be ready when the time comes."

They waited patiently on the landing outside number 12 apartment with chisels in their hand and a pot of adhesive ready in case they were approached by one of the residents and needed to explain what they were doing there. The two men knew that as soon as the door opened they would seize the opportunity to enter. They were so close to their goal and knew that once they were inside the apartment it would be only a question of waiting for the morning.

Inside number 12 a woman in her mid-forties carefully adjusted her hair, checked her handbag and gave a final glance in the mirror. Satisfied that everything was in order she moved towards the door and prepared to leave. She switched off the wireless in the flat and began moving towards the door. Looking at each other, Siegel and Carmona adjusted their neckerchiefs and pulled them up over their faces.

She opened the door and stepped outside, preparing to close it behind her when the two men rushed her. Siegel immediately placed his hand over her mouth and pushed her back inside the apartment. Carmona quickly grabbed the toolboxes and fetched them inside before closing the door behind him.

The woman was struggling to break free and in spite of her small stature and plumpness she was putting up a spirited fight. She tried to scream for help but only muffled sounds came from her mouth. Carmona saw the irony of an overweight Italian woman trying to fight with one of the most feared gangsters in America.

Sensing that Siegel was becoming frustrated by her resistance and might start using violence against the woman, he reached into his toolbox and took out a piece of rag. Approaching her quickly he grabbed her right wrist and with his other hand gestured to Siegel to remove his own hand from the woman's mouth. As he did so the woman prepared to scream but Carmona silenced her cries abruptly, pushing the rag into her mouth to make a crude gag before she had a chance to utter a sound. Still holding the woman's wrists Carmona pointed to the rope in the toolbox. Siegel produced it and quickly Carmona tied the woman's legs and wrists together. Although she was now securely fastened and silenced her eyes darted fire at the two men and she still tried vainly to release herself from her bonds.

As she lay on the floor both men looked around to see if she was on her own. Carmona came across a walk-in pantry and the two men picked her up and carried her into it. Just before he left her he spoke quietly to the woman in Italian.

"If you are still and quiet nothing bad will happen to you."

Her initial trauma was still clearly visible on her face but the eyes were beginning to be dominated by the emotion of fear. Carmona smiled at her in what he hoped was a reassuring way and came closer to the woman. As he did so she flinched and tried to move away, clearly expecting the worst from the two intruders.

"Signora, it is not you we want. You have no need to be alarmed. We will not hurt you as long as you remain still and quiet. Do not look upon us as bandits. We only need the use of your apartment for twenty-four hours. After the time is up you will be released unharmed."

The rooms in the apartment were huge with frescoed ceilings, thick walls and tiled floors. The drawing room was particularly elegant with French windows leading out on to a balcony. The sun was streaming in through the lace curtains and bounced off the large crystal chandelier that hung from the centre of the ceiling, casting rainbow patterns on the cream walls. Siegel studied the antique furniture and paintings on the walls.

"This broad's got class."

They went through the apartment methodically with their first priority being to see if the woman lived alone or had a husband who might come back at any time. After careful examination they saw nothing but clothes, perfume and make-up typical of a woman her age.

"Looks like it's just her," said Siegel with considerable relief. "It could have made our job a lot more difficult if we had to worry about someone else — especially a husband."

"Let's search her handbag and see if we can find the keys that open the gate leading into the back garden."

Carmona picked up the handbag lying on the floor and soon distinguished the key opening the door to the apartment from the one allowing them to leave through the back gate and slip away through the garden into the street outside.

As they approached the French window cautiously Siegel's hand went towards the door handle to open it but Carmona stopped him with a gesture.

"Not yet. We're going to have to crawl out there. We don't want anyone seeing us and wondering who we are or what we're doing in this woman's apartment. Stealth and silence, that's what we need. "

He opened the window and the two men crawled outside on their stomachs to get to the balcony. They knew this was how they would have to carry out the shooting tomorrow so it was good practice as well as making them invisible to people in the road below. The two of them made a thorough survey of the area. They observed the street below and examined the balcony for possible obstacles. The two men also looked for objects that might provide cover for them while they prepared for the assassination. First of all they laid down some mats from the kitchen and pushed the now empty wooden toolboxes to the front of the balcony. Tomorrow they would use them to give their rifles a steady base to rest on.

Some geranium plants were pushed to one side and rearranged to give them a clear view of the street. Peering through the wrought iron railings camouflaged by a large purple cistus bush and trailing plants they saw that the cover was good. The view of the street from the balcony was excellent and unobstructed.

"We need to get ourselves lined up in the best possible position before we get the rifles set up tomorrow morning."

After they had established their vantage points and memorized the positions in their minds Carmona looked at his watch before the two of them slowly crawled back inside the apartment on their stomachs.

As they settled down to wait for morning both men began reflecting upon their lives. Each knew tomorrow might be their last day on earth and they considered the strange sequence of events that had led them to this lonely destiny, perched in an apartment in Rome waiting to murder the most powerful man in Europe.

Siegel felt a mounting sense of excitement. The magnitude of what they proposed to do became clearer in his mind as the time for action was rapidly approaching. Turning to Carmona, he raised an issue that was troubling him.

"What happens if we pull it off?"

Carmona was surprised by that question

"Hitler will be dead and the world a better place."

"But what about — reprisals? Pogroms? The Nazis are bound to blame it on the Jews and then who knows what might happen?"

"Don't worry about that. Let's just focus on the job in hand. The politicians can sort out the mess later. We know what we came here for so let's just do it!"

Siegel stared through the now closed French window into the distance. He was like a tiger waiting for the moment to approach his prey and strike for the kill.

"When it's over I think I might try to change my life. It's not fair to Esta that she's always worrying if one day I won't come home and she'll be a widow and my kids orphans. The last few years I've been thinking about making a fresh start in Hollywood. I know a lot of people in the industry and I've got the looks and presence to be a movie star. What about you?

"You're young. You could make it work. At my age I just want a simple life. Half past eight at night," he said. "We'd better get some sleep. We need to be up around 5 in the morning to get ourselves set up. All we can do now is wait until tomorrow."

***

Across town Genovese was busy putting the finishing touches to his own plans. He had already assigned the gunmen who would accompany Moretti to the warehouse to kill Siegel and his accomplice.

"Nothing more we can do now," he said, turning to his *consigliore*. "It's a waiting game until they show up at the warehouse tomorrow afternoon."

Bellini was relieved that the first day of Hitler's visit had passed without incident. Either the huge police and military presence had deterred the Mafia from making their attempt on Mussolini's life or else they planned to carry out the assassination on another day.

20

Bellini hardly slept during the long night, his rest troubled by dark dreams in which he saw Mussolini shot by the assassins and his efforts to protect his country's leader in vain. When he finally woke and gazed into the mirror he saw bloodshot eyes staring back at him and his face was haggard and drawn. Glancing at the clock in his office he saw that it was half past six in the morning.

Briefly glancing at the itinerary for the day he identified the moment of greatest danger as taking place around ten in the morning. At that time Mussolini and Hitler would both be riding through the residential streets of Rome in an open car. There were many possible vantage points from which snipers could take aim — apartment blocks, shops, and balconies. The police had tried to identify them all but the Mafia were efficient, ruthless and devious enough to find a way of bypassing all his stringent security precautions.

There might even be traitors within the police and army who would assist them in return for money or other inducements. He gazed at the files on his desk, looking for some blinding revelation to leap out at him. If only he could identify the killers and eliminate them before they had time to strike.

Varese still languished in the cells and although he remained the best chance of finding any kind of meaningful lead Bellini doubted that the young man had any more information to give him. It was not even his

Don who had arranged to help the assassins and Mancini appeared to have vanished from sight with most of his followers. All he could do was hope a lucky break might come his way or the killers might become overconfident and show their hand prematurely.

Carmona made coffee when they woke. As usual Siegel was more talkative than his companion.

"Shut up and meditate or do your nails or something. You're getting on my nerves right now. Try and be quiet, can't you? This is the big day and I don't want us to screw up because of your big mouth."

"There's no way we'll screw up. The stakes are too high and we've done all we can. No one knows we're here."

He realised why Siegel had to be an integral part of the assassination plan but still wished he had either been allowed to carry out the scheme on his own or with a more reliable partner. He had been a liability from start to finish and if they succeeded in killing Hitler and getting away he hoped he would never set eyes on him again.

Carmona checked on the woman in the pantry.

"She's sound asleep; a few more hours and she'll be found."

In the living room he and Siegel assembled and loaded their sniper rifles. Physically and mentally both men were as prepared for their mission as they would ever be and now only time itself stood between them and a date with destiny.

"Three hours to go," Carmona said. "We'll make our way on to the balcony at half past nine and lay there until the time comes. Even then you don't fire until I give the signal."

Carmona concentrated on making sure that every aspect of the guns was right. The two men practised sighting and taking aim a number of times before he was satisfied that even the impatient Siegel would follow orders and shoot at their target with precision.

Taking off their workmen's clothes, they now wore their suits and could pass as ordinary office workers, salesmen or clerks once they were outside in the streets of Rome. Only the pistol each man wore within his shoulder holster made them different.

"Passport and money in your pockets?"

Siegel patted his suit to show they were both there.

"We'd best put on our gloves before we go outside. After it's over we'll take them off."

Carmona looked at his watch and gave a glance towards the window.

"Nearly time."

At the prospect of action Siegel roused himself. He was now alert and purposeful, all the spoilt self-indulgence that normally characterized him vanishing as if he'd taken off a heavy overcoat and handed it to the cloakroom attendant.

At 9.30 Carmona and Siegel cautiously opened the French windows and crawled on to the balcony. The two men lay flat on their stomachs and anxiously surveyed the scene below them. There were thousands of people filling the streets or leaning expectantly out of the windows of their homes. Carmona noted that all the spectators seemed to be dressed in their best clothes as they prepared to welcome their country's leader and his closest foreign ally. The women in the crowd were waving white handkerchiefs and everyone seemed to be holding a small swastika flag. They stood shoulder to shoulder in the street, their arms stretched out in the fascist salute. The smiling faces and cheering voices waited patiently to welcome their leader and Hitler.

The police lined the pavements and the presence of the army was also visible. Bellini sat in the motorcade gazing anxiously about for any possible hint of trouble. He saw nothing to make him suspect the presence of the assassins, but he knew that they were out there and that the motorcade was the most likely point of danger for the two dictators.

As the church bells struck ten the band began to play. The crowd went wild with excitement as they realized the music signalled the imminent approach of Mussolini and Hitler.

From the balcony Carmona gazed intently at the press of people and was almost overcome with disgust as he saw the enthusiasm on their faces. He could not understand how two men he regarded as brutal clowns could possibly enjoy such popularity. His throat tightened as the sheer audacity of their mission threatened to weaken his resolve at the very last moment.

Get a grip on yourself, he thought. I'm supposed to be the clear-headed one holding it together. I've been carrying Benny from start to finish and if I fall apart the mission will fail.

Siegel pointed into the near distance.

"They're coming down the street. Any minute now he'll be in front of us."

The two men fell silent as they gazed at the cheering crowd. On the balcony of the apartment both men lay with their rifles in position. With painstaking care and infinite patience they waited for the moment each had anticipated for so long.

Carmona felt a trembling in his limbs, dryness in his throat and a rapid acceleration in his heartbeat. His arms felt unsteady and even the position of the rifle against his shoulder felt looser than it should be. His breath came faster, in short almost gasping pants, as the tension built within him and adrenalin began to flow inside his body.

The car entered the street at last and the faces of the two men could be seen indistinctly from the balcony. Siegel and Carmona gazed at each other and then returned to scanning the procession.

"This is it, Luigi."

Both men strained with utter concentration upon the car carrying the two leaders slowly along the street with what seemed like an eternity of small steps. As Hitler came within range Siegel raised his rifle. He focused along its telescopic sights and saw the face of Hitler.

A morbid curiosity came upon him and he held that image in his vision, letting it imprint itself inside him with the clarity of a photograph. He had only been a figure glimpsed on posters or seen on newsreels but now, peering down on to the street from a balcony in Rome, he saw his enemy in the flesh.

Siegel noticed the piercing, hypnotic eyes but was most struck by the expression of euphoria upon Hitler's face. *I'll wipe away that smug look. I've got the power of life and death over you. At least I get to see your face before I kill you. You ugly fucking bastard, it's payback time for you.*

Tensing his body, his trigger finger nestled in readiness as Carmona shouted.

"Now!"

Above the sound of the cheering crowds his voice was hardly audible but Siegel, lying beside him on the balcony, heard and understood. Both men had Hitler in their sights and in the merest millisecond squeezed the trigger of their rifles. The silencers deadened the sound but the trajectory of the bullets could not be disguised.

The first shots scored a direct hit but both men still fired again. As people who were expert at handling guns they knew you always fire twice.

In the car Hitler's head exploded as the bullets smashed bone and parts of his brain oozed out. Blood spattered the other occupants of the car and Mussolini ducked on to the floor in search of cover. Hitler's chest sprayed out blood like a fountain and the gleaming buttons on his military tunic were stained dark as berries with his blood. The impact of the bullets threw him backwards and he fell heavily onto the seat of the car, all dignity departed from him as he lay there in his final seconds of existence. The death rattle in his throat was the last sound he made before eternal silence and darkness closed in upon him.

Only the thought that the gunmen might have missed their intended target and still meant to kill him, kept Mussolini inside the car, hiding from the public he had been so eagerly smiling at and waving to only a minute before. As the Duce crouched in the vehicle pandemonium raged all around him.

A few moments the streets had been filled with the happy laughing voices of the crowd. The flags and banners were waved and every face was wreathed in smiles.

Now it was as if all Rome was screaming. The enthusiasm and joy of the crowd had turned to wails and cries of fear. Tears fell from the faces of many who for a moment stood in stunned immobility as they gazed into the scene of carnage. In an instant, as if a film playing in slow motion returned to normal speed, the statue-like stillness of the crowd ceased.

The people who had been rooted to the ground in a paralysis of fear recovered the use of their legs at last. Their brains transmitted only a single overwhelming imperative message which a few seconds later was vocalized by a middle-aged man.

"Run!"

In seconds every member of the crowd was doing exactly that. They did not even seek to direct their flight but simply ran from the scene of the crime with the momentum and irresistible force of a river breaking its banks and flooding the plains below.

When he saw the bullets striking Hitler, Bellini froze. For all his precautions and the tight security, somehow the killers had managed to strike. He knew that all he could do now was try to avenge the slaying. His years of training helped him to keep his wits about him as he issued his orders to his men.

"Find the assassins!"

His mind was racing as he tried to rewind the film of the last few minutes in his mind. The shots must have come from a balcony on the left-hand side of the street. He needed to send armed officers in that general direction but there were a number of possible vantage points from which the snipers could have taken aim.

Something doesn't add up. Those two men were professional snipers and they got a direct hit on their target. If they had been aiming at Mussolini he would be dead now and that can only mean that Hitler was the intended target all along. Why would the Mafia want to kill Hitler? They had no quarrel with him.

"How is Il Duce?" he asked one of his men.

"He is unharmed," the officer replied. "We have taken him out of here to a place of safety."

"Good. Is Herr Hitler dead?"

"Yes."

Bellini returned to the business of directing the police in the areas where he wanted the search to be concentrated. His task was made harder by the press of people thronging the streets and running away in panic after what they had seen that day. All his efforts to establish some kind of orderly evacuation were fruitless as the crowds swarmed desperately in all directions.

The fact that it was Hitler rather than Mussolini who had been killed continued to trouble him. It was true that Hitler had plenty of enemies but not in Italy. *Who in our country could want to assassinate him?*

As he continued to try and direct his officers he saw Captain Solanio approaching. The man's grim face looked at Bellini with a mixture of anger and bafflement.

"Any progress?" he asked, his breath coming in short pants.

"Not yet."

"No sign of the killers?"

"No, but they can't have gotten very far with all these people about. My guess would be that they fired from the balcony of an apartment and then lost themselves in the crowd. Of course we'll try and find them but we don't know who they are or what they look like."

"There's going to be hell to pay with our German friends. Thank God it wasn't Il Duce!"

Bellini reflected that even though the situation was bad for him and his men it would have been far worse if it had been Mussolini lying dead in the car.

"What now?"

"God knows. It's totally chaotic at the moment. Just do what you can."

The captain got back into his squad car and drove off. Bellini could do little more than wait for the crowds to clear and begin searching top floor apartments with balconies. He knew it had to be done even though the assassins would be long gone by the time his men discovered their hiding place.

21

Siegel and Carmona crawled back inside the apartment, leaving their rifles and toolboxes behind on the balcony. Carmona left the apartment door wide open so that the woman hostage could be rescued. He looked at Siegel and made a sign for him to follow. They walked calmly down the metal fire escape that led into the garden. .

A blast of cold air filled their lungs as they made their way through the foliage. Moving quickly through the garden they heard the screams and wailing of the people outside. As they came to the garden gate, Carmona produced the key from his pocket. He opened it and then threw the key into a nearby bush.

They moved forward and joined the seemingly inexhaustible stream of panicking people. Everyone seemed to be lost in their own dark thoughts and stared around them wildly with faces drained of all expression. The stampeding crowds helped them melt away into an anonymous mass. A tide of fleeing bodies packed the street, all seeking escape from the scene of violent horror that had unfolded before them so unexpectedly that morning.

Carmona led the way and Siegel never took his eyes off him for fear of becoming separated. It was difficult to avoid stumbling and falling and being squashed flat against walls. People lunged frantically in search of an avenue of escape and the whole situation had passed completely out of control. In the utter confusion it took all their concentration to remain focused but at last they began to break free from the mass of people and strike out on their own.

Carmona instinctively led Siegel through side streets and narrow alleyways as the two men hurried towards their destination. The physical and mental effort was draining both men but their determination to escape and survive drove them on in spite of it.

At last the crowds were dispersing as they reached the suburbs of Rome. Coming to a small drinking fountain both men paused, exhausted, breathless and in a state of high mental agitation. They gratefully slurped the cold water into their parched throats and splashed their hot faces with the cool liquid.

"We did it!" Siegel spat out in a voice that, though weak, still rang with passion. "We killed the son of a bitch!"

"Now all we have to do is make it back home."

Still shaking from their ordeal the two men tried to walk as normally as they could. The last thing they wanted to do was to behave in a way that might attract unwelcome attention from the police.

In the distance they heard the sound of police sirens echoing round the ancient buildings and the noise of a thousand running footsteps which could be heard but no longer seen. The people of Rome took refuge in their homes, barricading all the windows and doors. Hitler was dead but the panic his death had brought made them hide away until they were certain that it was safe to venture outside again.

"The warehouse is only a short walk," Carmona said.

The two men approached their appointed rendezvous, a site that had been earmarked for development but where most of the buildings still lay empty.

Carmona scrutinized the area from a discreet distance and pointed to a warehouse.

"This is where we're supposed to meet Mancini's men. But just in case we've been betrayed we'd better find a place to hide. We'll hold back and watch before we make our move."

"What if no one turns up?"

Carmona gazed thoughtfully into the distance and did not answer. His trained eyes identified a wooden shed that was close enough to the warehouse to give them easy access if all was well but also offered cover and concealment if things went wrong.

"How are we going to make it back to America if the plan fails? Mancini's men were supposed to take us to the coast and put us on a freighter. If they don't turn up — or if they betray us — we could be stuck here for nothing. Or even wind up dead."

"If that happens, we'll have to find our own way back. But let's not get ahead of ourselves. We need to take cover inside that shed and wait."

The two men made their way towards the shed with extreme caution. As soon as they reached it, they drew their pistols. The men opened the door and nothing met their eyes beyond a couple of crates and a few undisturbed cobwebs. Closing the door behind them, they sat down on the wooden crates. The fastidious Siegel brushed away the dust from the box before he sat down.

"All we can do now is wait."

They lit cigarettes and inhaled deeply. As the smoke filled their lungs they began, if not exactly to relax, at least to recover from the ordeal of the last twenty-four hours. They did not speak as both men reflected on what had happened and Siegel fingered the gun in his holster in a nervous manner.

"Why don't they hurry up and come?"

"My guess is that they will come. Either Mancini's managed to organize our escape in spite of the difficulties or we've been betrayed. And if we've been sold out don't you think they'd send a welcoming party for us so they can get their hands on the reward money?"

In the distance they heard the sound of a car approaching. Both men inside the shed were instantly alert. Siegel fingered his pistol almost lovingly and gazed through the window as the car drew up. It was a black Fiat 508 Balilla limousine and Siegel was now in full readiness to fight or be evacuated to safety depending on the nature of the new arrivals.

"This is either Mancini's men or a set-up," he whispered. "If it's a set-up, we'll get them!"

The car parked and the men slowly got out and began making their way towards the warehouse. A glint of sunlight shone on the metal of the revolvers the men from the car were carrying. Their faces could be seen clearly now and Siegel reacted as he saw them approaching.

"Moretti. The bastard has sold us out for the reward money. I know one of those guys from when he was in America. He's one of Genovese's top trigger men."

Carmona was not surprised by the news. The size of the reward on offer was enough to strain the loyalty of most Mafiosi.

"What now?" he asked.

Siegel smiled, confident of his own ability to take control of the situation.

"Watch and learn. This is my territory!"

As the men approached the door of the warehouse and prepared to open it Siegel burst out of the shed like a sprinter, the much slower Carmona emerging a few seconds later. Both men had their revolvers cocked and ready and Siegel fired instantly.

Two of the men were hit in the back and fell on to the hard ground. The other two scrambled behind the car and took cover, firing shots as they ran but missing both men.

"Come out and fight!" Siegel yelled at them.

Carmona was amazed at the swiftness and dexterity with which Siegel fired his pistol. He had not managed to loose a single shot himself so far and was well aware that this time it was Siegel who was the senior partner.

Shots came from behind the car but Siegel scampered to one side and returned fire. Carmona tried to take cover but out in the open he was exposed and there were few obvious locations to conceal himself.

Bullets thudded into the car as Siegel and Carmona duelled with the men on the other side of the vehicle. The windshield was smashed and two tyres punctured as bullets hit them. Another bullet passed through the side window of the car.

Siegel was like a force of nature as he yelled at the remaining gunmen. He knew that one was Moretti and the other one was Genovese's top hit man. His grip tightened on the barrel of his gun as he clenched his teeth and shook with the primal rage surging through him as he stalked his prey. The adrenalin rush filling him as he closed in upon the enemy gave him an effortless ease of movement and speed of reaction although he knew he would pay for it later He was physically and emotionally exhausted after killing Hitler and only his professionalism held him together.

The men had been firing at each other for some time now and their pistols were empty. They needed to reload but neither side knew how much ammunition their adversaries had left. Reloading their weapons was the most dangerous part of the whole operation. In a cat and mouse game each took out fresh ammunition from their pockets, loaded the bullets into their revolvers quickly and hoped it would be fast enough to save their lives.

Siegel had become so focused upon Genovese's man that he had neglected to observe Moretti closely enough. Suddenly the other man fired but not at him. It was Carmona who was in the line of fire and Siegel raced across and pushed him aside roughly.

As he fell face forward on the ground Carmona tasted the dirt in his mouth. Spitting it out he saw Siegel whirling around and aiming his gun. He planted a bullet squarely in the centre of Moretti's head. The contents of his brain spilt out on to the ground and for the first time since the fight had begun Genovese's men were outnumbered.

Carmona rose to his feet and surveyed the area. *Only one man left now.* There was a sudden stillness as both Siegel and Genovese's man searched for an opening.

Trying to help his partner Carmona fired a shot towards the car. Genovese's man fired back and Siegel closed in for the kill.

Three shots rang out, two of them coming from Siegel's gun. There was a thud on the ground and then a long silence. Cautiously the two men investigated the scene but there was no doubt that all four of their adversaries were now dead. The area around their bodies was awash with blood and the stench of the gasoline and powder from the guns almost overpowering.

"You saved my life out there, Benny," Carmona said.

"We're a team, Luigi. I did what I had to do, that's all."

"Where did you learn to shoot like that?"

"Cowboy flicks," Siegel grinned.

Carmona was startled by that for a moment and then relaxed. *Let's hope the worst is over now. I know we still have to find another way out but I'm hoping that Bill will come good for us.*

"Come on, let's go. There's a church not far from here where we can rest up and make plans."

22

Mussolini, once he had recovered from the shock of Hitler's assassination, shouted at everyone within earshot.

"Call together the members of the Fascist Grand Council immediately! We need to discuss the new situation. Order the Bersaglieri on to the streets of Rome at once! Call the head of OVRA [the Fascist intelligence agency] and send him to meet me. Tell military intelligence to begin researching any possible foreign involvement in the assassination. And ring the chief of police and get him to see me!'

Soon the streets of Rome were filled with soldiers and police. Immediately noticeable was the presence of the Bersaglieri, the Italian Special Forces, marked by their wide-brimmed moretto hats with black capercaille feathers flowing down the right side. On their collars they wore double-tailed patches with the star of Savoy, symbolizing the flame of eternal Rome. Their brown boots were not polished but greased and the sight of these elite troops on the streets brought at least a sense of reassurance that things would soon return to normal. Their daggers glinted in the afternoon air as they rode around the city on their motorcycles, searching out the enemy.

Street by street, house by house, apartment by apartment, the police began their painstaking attempts to track down the killers. Rome was swamped with police, soldiers and agents of the intelligence services, all trying to comb the city inch by inch.

The scent of fear was palpable throughout Rome. Even though Hitler was dead an air of panic and confusion lay over everything. The soldiers and police officers were nervous, impatient and increasingly desperate as they continued their frantic pursuit of the assassins.

By now both Bellini and Solanio had been summoned to meet the Chief of Police in Rome, Arturo Bocchini. Having begun by giving both men a severe dressing down for allowing the assassination to take place, he then demanded to know what progress had been made in tracking down the killers.

"We had information that the Mafia planned to assassinate Il Duce but we had no idea that Hitler was a target," Bellini told him. "All our Mafia suspects have denied any knowledge of such a plan. At present we have no leads and we are not even certain from which apartment the fatal shots were fired. Even now the police are searching apartments with balconies in the Via Florio."

"Do you believe you can find the men responsible?"

"I think so, sir. But it will not be a quick process. We and the army have set up road-blocks and effectively sealed off Rome from the outside world. They cannot have escaped from the city and sooner or later we will find them."

"Solanio? Do you have any further information for me?"

"Sadly, sir, no. All we can do is persist in our search and seal off all the exits from Rome until we catch whoever is responsible for the assassination."

"Well, speed it up. I'm catching flak from Il Duce and half the government right now!"

Before long almost every known anti-fascist and anti-Nazi in Rome had been rounded up. Teams of police officers began questioning them about their movements, their associates and every aspect of their activities over the previous week.

Bellini was becoming weary of the seemingly endless round of interrogations. The more he questioned people and the more he sifted through the evidence the clearer it became to him that the assassination of Hitler was not a home-grown plot but had been masterminded from abroad.

It remained a mystery to him who was responsible and why. He understood that Hitler had many enemies but the organization of the killing baffled him. Clearly there must have been some kind of Mafia involvement and he knew already that the high-powered rifles used to carry out the assassination had been stolen from an army barracks in Rome. The person responsible for the theft might be caught but it was doubtful if he knew anything more than the order to steal the weapons.

If the killing had been planned abroad, who were the likely suspects? Soviet Russia? Spanish Republicans? Czechoslovakia, already engaged in a high-profile dispute with Germany over the Sudetenland? Anti-Nazi exiles?

Bellini was still analysing the possible culprits when the phone rang.

"Yes?"

"Sir, we have found a woman in her apartment. She says she was attacked by two men who held her prisoner and we have found two high-powered rifles on her balcony."

"Is she well enough to be questioned?"

"She is in shock but otherwise unharmed."

"Then I will meet with her immediately."

He grabbed his hat and coat and drove off to meet the woman. This could be the best chance of solving the case quickly.

He hoped that interviewing the woman who had been overpowered by the two men might lead to a breakthrough in the case. Unfortunately she knew little. The men who seized her wore neckerchiefs over their faces so she could not identify them when shown a series of photographs of know criminals or even provide sufficient detail for an artist's impression. One man was tall and the other short. She thought one was British or American and the other Italian. They spoke English but although she recognized the language she did not speak it and couldn't understand what the two men were saying.

He examined the forensic evidence the police team had gathered painstakingly from the scene of the crime. The rifles, toolbox and workmen's clothes had all been analyzed but the two killers had worn gloves and there was no fingerprint evidence that might link them to known criminals. Neither domestic records nor the resources of Interpol were able to furnish him with the slightest clue as to their identity.

Cursing the absence of any substantial leads, he wondered how he could possibly come up with any kind of meaningful statement to the media about progress in the case. He was already in a foul temper as the spectre of a high-profile assassination that looked increasingly unlikely to be solved haunted him when the phone rang.

"Yes? What is it?"

The news on the other end of the line at least provided an almost welcome distraction from what seemed like an increasingly futile police investigation into Hitler's death. Four bodies had been reported as being found outside a warehouse in a development area and all the victims appeared to have been shot. *More Mafia gang wars, Bellini thought irritably. It must just be coincidence or is there a connection?*

He made his way to the scene of yet another murder where he and his men examined the area carefully, photographing everything, removing bullets that had missed their intended targets and finally arranging for the dead men to be taken to the mortuary for identification and analysis.

There had obviously been a gun battle between the four dead men and an unknown number of killers ranged against them. The men who had survived the encounter had clearly escaped on foot as there was no sign of any other vehicle besides the Fiat out of which the four dead men had emerged.

A thought struck him as he considered the situation carefully. *Perhaps there was a tie-in between the assassination and the mayhem he saw before him. The men might have been meant to rendezvous with the killers here but decided to double-cross them for the reward money. A bloody shoot-out had followed and the two assassins somehow overcame the odds and walked away from the scene alive.*

Where would they go after the gunfight, though? The isolation of the areas was obviously one of the reasons it would have been chosen as a rendezvous point. He began considering possible sites to which they might have made their way after the gunfight was over in the hope that a search of those areas might help him get a handle on the movements of the killers.

23

Eva Braun was in her hotel room trying on a new outfit that she had purchased the previous day from one of the most luxurious stores in Rome. She meant to show it off to Hitler when he returned from his state duties later.

She heard the cheering crowds and saw the flags waving. The streets were awash with a press of people. *I'm so proud of him, she thought. And he's all mine!*

It was only a few minutes after Siegel and Carmona had fired the fatal shots that an ashen-faced messenger came to the hotel. Himmler and Goebbels and Hess were all inside and they first received the news.

An utter stillness fell upon them as the news of the assassination slowly sank in. Himmler was the first to recover and immediately ordered his SS bodyguard to go out on to the streets of Rome and track down the killers. Hess sat in his chair, wide-eyed and still unable to comprehend the horror of the news he had just received. Goebbels watched the streets outside, wishing to be avenged on Hitler's killers but utterly powerless to do so.

In Eva's room the telephone rang. One of the few people in Hitler's entourage who knew her true status as his mistress spoke to her. His voice was trembling and he almost mumbled the news.

"The Führer is dead," he told her. "Murdered. Assassinated. I am sorry, Fräulein Braun."

Eva did not take in the news at first and thought she had misheard. She made the man repeat his message.

A sudden wailing sprang out of her throat and tears flowed from her eyes, gushing down her powdered cheeks. *This is beyond any pain I have known before. The man I love has been murdered here in Rome and nothing in life matters any longer.*

She staggered across to the bed and buried her head in the pillow, tearing at the pillows and bed linen with her fingers and hands.

All that gave meaning to my life is gone, she thought. He was the centre of my world and now only a gaping void yawns open where my heart was. Adolf is dead. What reason do I have for living?

She eyed a bottle of sleeping pills at the side of the bed. Eva went into the bathroom and turned on the tap. Filling a glass with water, she carried the tumbler across to her bedside table. Her hands trembled slightly as she opened the bottle and took out the entire contents.

If I die now, she thought, either I find oblivion in death or I will be reunited with Adolf in the afterlife. She wrote a farewell letter addressed to her family and left it by the side of her bed. Picking up the tablets, she put them inside her mouth and washed them down with the water.

It was some hours before anyone came into Eva's room. When the hotel maid appeared at first she thought Eva was sleeping. Then she saw the empty bottle of pills and screamed. The hotel manager was fetched and then Himmler entered the room.

He saw at once what had happened and he knew why. One of the few people who knew about Hitler and Eva Braun, he opened the letter to her family and read it carefully. Satisfied that there was nothing within it that could harm the Führer's reputation, he placed it back inside the envelope.

"An accidental overdose," he said to the hotel manager. "I will get one of my own doctors to certify the cause of death."

"As you wish, Herr Himmler."

The manager wanted to avoid any hint of scandal or any suggestion of suicide. *It's crazy enough in Rome at the moment, he thought. Let Himmler deal with it. I'm sure he's used to brushing things under the carpet.*

Himmler spoke quickly to one of his aides and asked him to take care of the matter before returning to the meeting room.

"Perhaps now," he said, "we should contact Mussolini and discuss the consequences of our Führer's tragic assassination."

24

Mussolini was expecting the Nazi leaders to contact him but he still dreaded the prospect of meeting them and having to explain how all his elaborate security precautions had failed. He had already convened an emergency meeting of the Fascist Grand Council where there had been some heated exchanges between himself and some other senior fascists. Dino Grandi had been particularly critical.

"I never wanted us to become friends with the Germans," he said angrily. "They were our enemies during the war and the Austrians have always been our enemy. And Hitler was an Austrian!"

Even Mussolini's son-in-law Galleazo Ciano was not encouraging.

"I fear that Hitler was dragging us into a war over Czechoslovakia. Perhaps his assassination may be a blessing in disguise. It will take time for the Nazis to sort things out back home and whoever takes over may be less willing to risk another world war."

Mussolini tapped his fingers on the desk to show his disapproval of his remarks.

"I served my country during the war. We have fought in Abyssinia and we are fighting in Spain. Our nation is a great power and we are the heir to the proud tradition of the Roman Empire. But there will never be another war like the Great War. Britain and France will not risk it and Stalin has enough to do maintaining himself in Russia."

"The other Nazi leaders will want to meet with you, Benito," said Grandi. "What will you tell them?"

Mussolini stood up and paced around the room.

"What can I tell them? Somehow — in spite of our precautions — an assassin struck. I have no idea who or why but someone will have to pay!"

"Do you imagine that Goering will be any less warlike than Hitler? Or if it's Hess — don't you think Himmler and Goebbels and Goering can manipulate him? Do you think the Nazis won't blame us for what's happened? And demand compensation from us?"

"What do you mean, compensation? I'm not to blame!"

"Well, if Hitler was prepared to go to war over the Sudetenland his successors may well demand that we return the South Tyrol. Or even northern Italy which in their version of history belongs to Germany because a long time ago it was the kingdom of Lombardy."

"That is impossible, Dino. I will never give up an inch of our sacred Italian soil. I'm looking to expand our empire — not to give up territory we already hold."

"Let's hope the Nazis see it that way."

"We need to have an agreed policy when you meet them," Ciano said. "How will you respond to Hess and the others?"

"I shall express my deep grief at Hitler's passing, of course. We will point out that we are doing everything in our power to track down the assassins but that as it was obviously a professional job it won't be easy. I've got all available police and paramilitary resources working on it and Rome's sealed up completely. They won't get away."

Ciano, on Mussolini's orders, rang the Nazi leaders. He was put through to the room where Hess answered the call. After the expected condolences Ciano came to the point.

"Would it be possible to meet with Il Duce? There is much to discuss."

"This afternoon we will be ready. Where shall we meet?"

"Perhaps Il Duce's office?"

"We will see you there. Herr Himmler, Herr Goebbels and Herr Ribbentrop will accompany me."

Ciano put the phone down and reported back to Mussolini.

"Let's hope Dino's wrong about their intentions," Mussolini said. "I don't want to fall out with the Germans."

25

Four hours after the assassination Hess, Goebbels, Himmler and Ribbentrop called an emergency meeting. They wore black armbands as a sign of mourning and SS guards stood outside the door of the room where the Nazi leaders gathered to discuss the new situation.

The window drapes remained closed and the portrait of Hitler on the wall was decked in black satin. Each one of them looked haggard, pale and still unable to believe or fully comprehend what had happened that day.

They moved towards the table with dignity and their heads held high. Hess was the first to speak.

"Our beloved Führer is dead. He was the savior of our nation. We will continue the struggle he began and spread National Socialism with equal fervour. Long live the Third Reich!"

"Heil Hitler!" came a chorus from around the table.

"We will continue the work of transforming Berlin into the largest and greatest city in the world and we will rename it Germania. There will be a huge mausoleum for him in Berlin. His sarcophagus will be laid to rest in Munich, the birthplace of our movement."

Goebbels responded enthusiastically to that idea.

"Adolf saw architecture as 'the word in stone' — he believed it could impart a specific message. Germania will be made out of granite and marble and quotations from *Mein Kampf* will be etched into the granite. The

Hall of the People will be twice the size of St Peter's Basilica in Rome and will fit up to 180,000 people."

The vision of the new Germania lifted their spirits slightly. Goebbels continued to try and make them look to the future.

"A five-mile boulevard will run north to south and an Arch of Triumph will carry the names of Germany's 1.9 million fallen during the war. The city will be filled with grand buildings and statues that as our beloved Führer proclaimed will last for a thousand years. The colossal dimensions of these works will overawe and intimidate the whole world!"

"Yes!" the normally reserved Himmler shouted. "When people are silent, stones speak."

Hess added his voice to the chorus.

"We will turn Linz, the Führer's birthplace, into one of the most beautiful cities in the Reich and transform it into the cultural capital of our empire. Art galleries and concert halls will be built dedicated to the Godfather of Linz as Adolf proclaimed himself only a few weeks ago when he visited Austria after the Anschluss."

Goebbels put into words the task that lay ahead of them.

"What we must do now is plan for the future — a Germany without our beloved Führer."

A moment of reflection followed his words before Hess spoke.

"We must move his body back home," he said. "A week — perhaps a month — of national mourning. And then a state funeral. Adolf wished to be buried in the Ehrentempel next to the Führerbau in Munich with his sarcophagus outside exposed to the elements as a visible and permanent memorial to his greatness. Let's honor his wishes."

Himmler took off his spectacles and polished them carefully before replacing them.

"Yes, I agree. It is of course my responsibility as head of the Gestapo and SS to track down the assassins and punish them. Perhaps we need to consider reprisals as I cannot believe whoever murdered our Führer acted alone. They must have had assistance both inside and outside Italy."

He paused for a moment to allow the effect of his words to sink in.

"Of course we cannot be certain how extensive the conspiracy is or how far-reaching its targets are. The four of us may well be in imminent danger of assassination and I believe we should return to Germany with all due speed."

Goebbels reacted at once to the suggestion of a wider conspiracy.

"The Jews are to blame for this, I suppose. Everywhere you look they try to destroy Germany!"

"That is possible. But we have many other enemies — the Communists, the Freemasons, the capitalists and the reactionaries. Any one of those groups could have been involved. I will discover the truth in due course but in the meantime it is essential that we return to Germany. We must fly back home with the Führer and let the rest of our party return by train."

Ribbentrop, the Foreign Minister, spoke for the first time.

"We must demand compensation for the assassination from Mussolini. The Italians must give us South Tyrol and the whole of northern Italy. It used to be the kingdom of the Lombards and it is time to return it to its rightful German owners."

Goebbels regarded Ribbentrop's comments as unhelpful and inappropriate. He tapped his feet under the table and wished he was not there at all. As Goering had once remarked scathingly, "he bought his title, married his money and cheated his way into the Party." *Goebbels remembered that he had described him as "an adventurer without principles" and once again he was showing no sense of decorum in the presence of grief.*

"Yes, let's grab back our land from the Italians," Ribbentrop said. "Why should we allow Mussolini to posture about his new Roman Empire when we're the Master Race and we're top dogs in Europe right now?"

Himmler inspected his glasses. *The appointment of Ribbentrop as Foreign Minister was one of Adolf's worst decisions, he thought.*

"Joachim, of course there must be some kind of — restitution — by the Italians for allowing this atrocity to occur on their soil. But we need to temper our natural grief and anger with caution and make only realistic demands upon Il Duce. It is possible that he might agree to cede the South Tyrol but he would certainly not agree to gift us the whole of northern Italy. To make such a demand upon him would mean that we would find ourselves in an immediate state of war with Italy."

Goebbels was the first to react to Himmler's words.

"What of it? What chance do you think the Italians would stand against us? The war would only last six weeks!"

"Five days!" said Ribbentrop.

Himmler was less sanguine about the prospect.

"They have a very fine air force. Nearly as good as our Luftwaffe. And they have a stronger navy than we do, at least in terms of surface vessels. In any event it is not simply a question of military considerations or the needless loss of German lives. The political implications of a war between Italy and Germany are not promising. At present the Italians and Poles are our only European allies and we cannot afford to alienate our friends."

"Friends?" Goebbels yelled. "They have allowed the Führer to be assassinated!"

"That is true, but we still need to remember that we were encircled during the war and that Italy was part of the coalition against us. There is also the additional consideration that if we go to war with Italy both our countries will have to withdraw our forces from Spain. That will lead to Franco's defeat as the Spanish Republicans, already receiving considerable military assistance from Stalin, would win the war. Instead of three fascist and National Socialist governments in Europe we would be left with only one. No, we cannot afford to go to war with Italy. Of course we would win such a conflict but at what cost? We must be prudent rather than reckless in this hour of danger."

Hess spoke quietly.

"Our nation has lost its greatest leader and I have lost my dearest friend. He saved our country from

Communism and rescued it from economic collapse. Our Führer was a friend to each one of us and we need to celebrate his life, grieve for his passing and preserve his legacy. This is no time to be talking about war. Let us return home with his body and let our nation and the world pay him the respect he deserves."

The unexpected assertiveness of Hess surprised the company. Goebbels and Himmler became reflective as they considered the changed situation.

"As Deputy Führer I am now the new leader of Germany," Hess said. "When we return to Germany I will convene a meeting of all our ministers and decide on the future of our country."

Goebbels and Himmler were already wondering how they could turn the new situation to their advantage. Each harboured ambitions for the leadership themselves and knew that the same was true of Goering in Berlin.

Himmler was the first to come to a decision.

"We must put aside everything else and bury our Führer. After we have done that we will consider the future of our nation. In the meantime the line of succession is clear and in accordance with the Führer's wishes I say, "Heil Hess!"

The unexpected salutation relieved the tension in the room. Goebbels, considering the best way to further his own ambitions, decided to move on with proceedings.

"The most sensible next step seems to be talking to Mussolini. Perhaps at this stage we should avoid mentioning the Tyrol or any other territorial claims."

26

When Mussolini met the Nazi leaders later there was none of the friendliness that had existed between himself and Hitler. He neither knew nor trusted the other four men and they were equally suspicious of him. After the formalities of condolences the serious business of the meeting began.

"Our concern with ill-treatment of German nationals in other countries is not restricted to those in the Sudetenland. Danzig, Memel, Eupen-Malmedy and Alsace-Lorraine are also areas needing to be liberated from foreign domination and restored to the Fatherland," Goebbels said.

"I would of course support Germany in all those territorial claims," Mussolini said.

"And of course there is the question of South Tyrol."

Goebbels' voice was quiet but the effect of his words was like a thunderstorm raging. Mussolini's bull-neck quivered and he clenched his fists, trying to control his anger.

"There is no South Tyrol question. The Führer assured me personally that he had no intention of seeking the return of that portion of our country. Or any part of Italy."

Mussolini was resolute and defiant as he faced the Nazi leaders. Ribbentrop responded to Mussolini's challenge.

"The new German government will decide what territorial claims it has upon other countries," he said sharply. "It is not your decision but ours!"

For a moment Himmler wondered if Mussolini was going to hit Germany's Foreign Minister. With a supreme effort of will he controlled himself.

"We have two nations joined together in friendship for the last three years," he said, "Why would you want to throw away our alliance? Germany is not exactly overburdened with friends at present."

Hess, as if slowly waking from a long dream, intervened.

"The Führer always spoke highly of you, Duce. He valued the friendship between our nations and so do I. There is no reason for our co-operation not to continue. We have fought side by side in Spain to establish fascism and we will continue to do so. I am sure that we can achieve a peaceful settlement with the Czechs but even if that is not possible your country is the last one we would go to war with."

His words immediately mollified Mussolini. Goebbels was surprised to hear such a sensible and decisive statement from Hess. Himmler seized the opportunity to offer some thoughts of his own.

"The Axis — the alliance between Italy and Germany," he said, "is of paramount importance. We both wish to see the triumph of Franco in Spain and on most other matters of foreign policy our goals are identical. It is essential that the cordial relations between us survive even the tragic assassination of the Führer."

Mussolini distrusted all four of the men sitting before him. Hess struck him as weak, Ribbentrop as an arrogant fool while Goebbels and Himmler were devious. Goering was not with the group but on previous encounters

Mussolini had not been impressed. He felt certain that there would be a struggle for power now that Hitler was dead and it was not at all clear what the consequences would be.

"I am sure that our alliance — our Pact of Steel — will remain unbroken in spite of the cowardly assassination of our mutual friend. I can assure you that I am devoting every single resource to tracking down Adolf's killers. They will not escape and they will be executed."

Relieved that his tense meeting with the Nazi leaders was over at last, Mussolini made his farewells. Hess and his colleagues prepared to return home while Mussolini began harassing the chief of police, demanding results.

27

The news of Hitler's assassination was telephoned through to Goering in Berlin. He had not been in the entourage that had visited Italy and had remained behind in temporary charge of Germany in the absence of the nation's leader. Now he sat at his desk, pondering the tragic events. He looked up at the portrait of Hitler that hung above and was filled with a genuine sense of sorrow.

Adolf, he thought, you weren't just our greatest leader and our country's savoir but you were my best friend.

He looked at the picture of Hitler again and began issuing orders.

"Let all portraits of the Führer be draped in black. Let the flags be hung at half-mast. Let the churches hold services in his memory."

Goering walked across to the window. On the streets below he could see crowds beginning to gather. The sound of wailing and tears filled the air and he knew at once that the whole nation was in mourning for its lost leader.

Adolf, your legacy lives on. We will carry on the flame of National Socialism and its brightness will not be dimmed even by your cowardly murder. The Third Reich that you have given us will last for a thousand years and will be the greatest empire ever seen on earth. All Germans will come together under our banner and the whole world will come to see the greatness of your vision.

Goering turned back and gave a final glance around his office in the Reich Chancellery. His grief was genuine and would never leave him but now was the time for resolute action.

"Send for Heydrich immediately!"

Reinhard Heydrich was young even by the standards of Nazi leaders. Still in his twenties, the blonde-haired, blue-eyed, tall man was considered by many to exemplify the ideal Aryan type. Heydrich played the part to perfection and was often considered a possible successor to Hitler in the distant future.

It was ironic that such an archetypal Aryan type harboured a dark secret. Heydrich was not his real family name, and his father had changed it before his son was born. His father's real name was not the Bruno Heydrich that he adopted, but Bruno Isidor Süss. Both Heydrich's parents were Jewish, a fact he was so desperate to conceal from the world that he vandalized the graves of his father and mother to destroy the evidence of his Jewish parentage.

Heydrich had kept his secret safe, only the indefatigably curious Himmler knowing the truth. Himmler recognized Heydrich's ability and never revealed his knowledge of Heydrich's Jewish origins to anyone. A false "Aryan" family tree was drawn up for him and he was appointed Deputy Leader of the SS and became one of the most powerful and feared men in Germany.

"Reinhard," Goering said quickly as he entered the office. "I assume you've heard the sad news about the Führer."

"Of course, Hermann. We are all stunned and grieved by this terrible event."

"I cannot believe the assassins acted alone. They must have had outside help. Round up all known dissidents and throw them in concentration camps. They will be questioned to see if any of them has guilty knowledge of the plan."

"Consider it done. Have you spoken with Hess or Himmler or Goebbels?"

"Not yet. I assume they'll be in touch shortly."

Heydrich left the Chancellery and began issuing orders to arrest thousands of people on the Gestapo and SS lists of suspected persons. *He wondered curiously if his position would change now that Hitler was dead. Obviously Hess or Goering would take over but he knew that both Himmler and Goebbels also harboured ambitions for the leadership as of course did Heydrich himself. There will be some interesting manoeuvring when they return from Rome. He smiled faintly.*

28

Within Germany itself all was confusion. The five most senior Nazi leaders had gone to Italy with Hitler and were virtually hiding away from the outside world. Goering, Bormann, Rosenberg and Heydrich were effectively running the country and Heydrich, Himmler's deputy, organized mass arrests of dissidents as soon as he heard the news.

Across Germany and Austria ordinary people wept in the streets. Angry crowds gathered outside the Italian Embassy in Berlin which had to be protected from attack by armed soldiers and SS men. German embassies across the world and all government buildings within the Reich flew the flag at half-mast. There was a sense of disbelief, of genuine grief and a sense of utter loss.

"Our Führer is gone," one member of the public told a foreign journalist. "He was our leader, the savior of our country. What will become of us now?"

Millions of Germans seemed unable to comprehend the enormity of what had taken place. Grown men and hardened veterans of the war wept in the streets. Huge bouquets of flowers were laid spontaneously outside public buildings by ordinary citizens. Work almost ceased and where it continued did so in a half-hearted, robotic manner.

The whole nation appeared to have lost its sense of purpose and its normal dynamism. It was as if they were an audience watching a play in which the hero had suddenly and unexpectedly been killed and they waited for the next act of the drama to unfold, somehow hoping vainly for the miracle of his rebirth.

29

Within a short time Siegel and Carmona found themselves entering the Church of Santa Maria. Sitting down on the wooden pews, they tried to compose themselves.

It was cool and dark within the church and a feeling of peace and drowsiness began to steal over them. Both men knew that they had to rest and recover their strength. They reflected on the past few hours. Neither man was religious but the solemnity of the place and the enormity of the events made them both say a silent prayer.

The stillness and their contemplation was interrupted suddenly by the sound of two women entering the church. A young woman in her twenties and a more mature woman dressed in floral cotton frocks with stylish straw hats set off with a gardenia took off their sunglasses and began looking around the church. When Siegel heard their American accents he perked up suddenly.

"I'll go to the rest room and spruce myself up," he told Carmona. "You go and talk to the two women. I need time to think."

He promptly disappeared and left Carmona alone in the church. The Italian made his way towards them and spoke.

"There has been heavy rain and the river may flood. We may need to evacuate people if it gets worse."

The two women scrutinized him for a moment before replying. Then the older one spoke.

"The plans for any necessary evacuation are already in hand."

A wave of relief washed over Carmona at these words. His contact in Rome had come good and he and Siegel were going to be rescued.

"Thank God. I wondered if Bill would come through for me."

"Well, he did. We've got everything arranged. Get Benny interested in us."

"That's easy," he said, looking straight at the younger woman. "He's a sucker for a pretty face."

Siegel returned looking cleaner and fresher. He had washed the grime from his hands and face, wetted and combed his hair and even rubbed down his suit with a damp cloth to remove the dust.

"Hi there, I'm Benny. I guess we must all be American tourists!"

"I'm Marianne," said the young woman. "This is my Aunt Celia. We've come over from Virginia on vacation."

Carmona took the opportunity to slip into the rest room at the back of the church leaving Siegel with the women.

"Are you enjoying your time in Italy? What do you think of Rome?"

"Well, I was really looking forward to my visit but now Hitler's been assassinated it's totally changed my mood. I'm terrified to be honest and as two women on our own I can't wait to get back home again!"

"Well, at least you ladies don't have to worry about that any more. You've got two strong men to look after you."

Marianne took Siegel by the arm and began showing him around the church. He tried to be attentive but all he wanted to do was charm the two women into letting them stay with them. Carmona joined them after a few minutes and the four of them chatted amicably. The strain was beginning to tell on Siegel and he knew that he had to get outside and clear his head.

"Anyone fancy a cigarette?" he asked.

The four of them stepped out into a blaze of sunlight and lit up their cigarettes. As he blew smoke into the air Siegel relaxed a little. They were some distance from the road but could hear the rumbling sound of army trucks passing and the wailing of police sirens. Sitting on a bench in the sanctuary rose garden the two men tried to regain their strength. They were both utterly exhausted and not in the mood to make polite conversation but it was difficult for them to remain silent.

"When are you going back to America?" Carmona asked.

"We're going back in three days' time on the *Conte di Savoia* from the port of Civitavecchia."

That piece of information made Siegel become animated. For all the excitement he felt at that news he was so tired that he could not stop himself yawning. Apologizing quickly he made the excuse that he was hungry.

"Well, in that case I suggest we all go back to our villa," said Celia. "A friend has let us stay there. All the restaurants will be closed but we can cook you a meal. My car's over there — shall we go?"

"Could you just let me have a few minutes to discuss things with my partner?" Carmona asked.

Celia agreed and both men strolled towards a high hedge where they could not be seen or heard.

"Well, Luigi, let's take these two broads up on their offer."

"We have no choice. Now that Mancini's men have gone to ground and Genovese is after us we must take shelter where we can find it. We have to get rid of our guns. If they find us with them we'll go right to the top of their list of suspects!"

They explored the garden and saw a small ornamental goldfish pond.

"Let's ditch our stuff in here."

The two men checked that no one else was in the vicinity before removing their equipment and watched it sink beneath the water. They saw the bubbles rising to the surface of the pond and a sense of relief came over them.

They took a short drive through the back roads before arriving at an ochre coloured villa that had been mellowed by the sun. The villa was secluded, surrounded by oaks and olive trees. A number of terraces with marble steps led up to the front door of the property. Celia took out the key and opened the door.

"Sit down and make yourselves at home. There's a bar over there."

Both men almost raced across to the bar and poured themselves a large bourbon while the two women disappeared into the kitchen to prepare a meal.

"God, I needed that!"

"Me too."

"You know, we have to trust these women. We've run out of options. We'll be safe here and we can rest up. That's all we can do right now," Carmona said.

"Yes, I can't believe our luck."

Wandering over to the bar they poured themselves another Bourbon and both men sprawled out on the sofa. Marianne tiptoed into the living room and saw them snoring soundly. She returned to the kitchen to talk things over with her companion.

"Are they both asleep?" Celia asked.

"Yes, they are."

"Thank God for that. We need to discuss the situation. Let's go into the garden so we won't be overheard."

The two women made their way into the small garden and stood beside a cypress tree. Celia began briefing the younger woman.

"We have to get those two back to America safely. Your job is to get Benny interested in you so he feels relaxed and trusts us completely."

"I can do that."

30

The two men slept for six hours before waking up in a darkened room. The metal shutters on the windows had been closed and the curtains drawn. The smell of cooking wafted in to them and excited their taste buds. Both men realized how hungry they were.

They felt refreshed after their sound sleep but still felt sticky and dirty. Making their way to the first floor bathroom they showered and with no clean clothes to wear they wandered into the bedroom next door stark naked.

Marianne knocked on the door and the men were startled and faintly embarrassed by their present state of undress. She put her head around the door with a smile on her face and quickly reassured them.

"There are some clothes in the wardrobe and I'm sure the owner won't mind you borrowing them."

The two men went through the wardrobe and selected various items of clothing. Carmona grumbled as he saw that most of the clothes would fit Siegel without any problem but did not hang so well on him.

The men dressed in flannel trousers, white shirts with a tie and a blazer. As they approached the dining room Celia gave Carmona a rapid glance and he excused himself for a moment.

"You go on in, Benny. Won't be a moment — bit of an upset stomach."

Siegel entered the dining room alone as Carmona headed towards the bathroom where Celia joined him. She turned on the water to disguise their rapid but secret conversation.

"This is how we'll play it. The two of you will come back with us on the *Conte di Savoia* in three days' time. Marianne will flirt with Benny and make him think she wants a romance. Otherwise he won't trust us. You and I will have to do the same or he'll get suspicious. We're both trained professionals so we know how to act a part. Is there anything else I need to know?"

"There might be a news item tomorrow about four Mafiosi shot dead at a warehouse."

"Good God, not more killing!"

"We were ambushed; we had no choice. It was them or us."

"Do you know who they were?"

"One worked for Mancini and was one of our bodyguards in the safe house. He obviously wanted the reward money. The other three worked for Genovese."

Celia digested the information and considered its ramifications.

"Will Genovese take action?"

"That's hard to say. If he goes to the police he is admitting being an accessory to mur

der. He may try and kill us at the port instead."

"We'll have to see about that. I may need to make special arrangements to prevent that from happening. I had better get back and start serving the meal. You go first."

He made his way to the dining room while Celia turned off the water and returned to the kitchen. She realized the crucial importance of putting on a front and making it appear perfectly natural that in three days' time they would sail back to America together. Analysis and planning were more her usual style within the service but she knew that in this instance a combination of acting skills and using her femininity as bait were essential tools for the success of the mission. She smiled in the kitchen, reflecting that it had been a while since that side of her personality had been called upon. In a strange way she was looking forward to playing the part.

The two men sat at the dining table looking much smarter and cleaner than a few hours earlier and feasted their eyes eagerly on the food before them. They ate their meal and engaged in conversation with the women. The evening passed pleasantly enough.

31

Genovese heard the news that Moretti and the three gunmen he had sent with him were all dead and realized it completely ruined his plans.

"Bastards!" he shouted. "How did they manage that? Where are they hiding now? Angelo, have Mancini's men taken them to a place of shelter?"

His *consigliore*, Angelo Maldini, shook his head vigorously.

"Mancini's people have gone to ground. None of them would risk sticking their neck out now after what's happened."

Genovese considered the situation.

"In a way that's good. It means that they must be hiding out on their own. And they can't go far so they must be somewhere in Rome or the suburbs. Put out a red alert and tell anyone who sees them to get in touch. In the meantime assemble a hit squad for me, Angelo. I want the ten best shooters we've got. This time there's going to be no mistakes. I want them both dead!"

Genovese then telephoned Bellini and told him it was imperative they met. "Not in your office. Somewhere we can talk undisturbed and without any fear of being overheard. Meet me at the Trevi Fountain in half an hour."

Bellini put the phone down and immediately realized the significance of the call. The men killed at the warehouse were sent by Genovese to murder the two assassins but had been killed themselves. *How am I supposed to co-operate with a man like that?*

For a moment he considered ignoring Genovese's suggested rendezvous but then a thought struck him. *If Genovese had sent his killers after the two assassins that could only mean he knew who they were and that they were expecting to be picked up, probably by Mancini's gang. Whether or not Mancini or one of his henchmen had sold the assassins out to Genovese was unclear but it meant he had a guilty knowledge which would put him in a difficult, even vulnerable, position.*

When the two men met Bellini prepared to go on the offensive.

"We have a few things to talk about, Lieutenant," said Genovese.

"Yes, I agree, Signor Genovese. For instance how did three of your men and a fourth whom I do not know become involved in a gun battle outside a warehouse?"

He spread his hands and his face assumed an expression of injured innocence.

"We were ambushed."

"But what were four armed men doing at an empty warehouse anyway?"

Bellini was determined to get something at least resembling a truthful answer out of the Mafia Don and would not let himself be intimidated by the man.

"Of course I was shocked when I heard the news, Lieutenant. It is tragic that our country's best friend should lose his life on a visit to our fair city of Rome. But I swear to you I had no hand in any such cowardly plot. I am a personal friend of Il Duce, Count Ciano and—"

"Yes, we know all about your connections. That isn't what interests me. Why did your men — including one we wanted to question about a number of unsolved murders — go to the warehouse in the first place?"

Genovese looked uncomfortable as he realized that Bellini could not be shaken off easily. He started off by trying to reassure him.

"Let me begin by giving you some information you will be most anxious to hear. As a civic minded person I felt it my duty to inform you —"

"Don't try and take me for a fool. You, an upstanding member of the community! Just give me this piece of information."

Genovese hesitated for a moment before continuing, still reluctant to give an even vaguely truthful answer.

"I know who the killers are."

"And you kept this information from me? That could be considered treason or at least accessory to murder!"

Genovese began to sweat as for the first time he sensed that his adversary had the upper hand. He was not accustomed to dealing with honest police officers and found it a considerable strain.

"I only discovered the truth this morning. A man from a rival — association — came to me and told me who they are."

"And of course instead of reporting the matter to me you chose to send gunmen after the assassins to try and collect the reward money. Who are the two killers?"

"I only know one of them. There was an older man with him — an Italian in his fifties called Luigi. The other man was Benny Siegel. Often known as "Bugsy" Siegel because he's plain mad."

Bugsy Siegel! Bellini had heard the name before and knew he was one of the most feared gangsters in America. Yes, he could imagine a man with his reputation wanting to kill Hitler. He was also Jewish which gave him an additional motive for the assassination.

My God, that's it. There never was a plot to kill Mussolini. The target had been Hitler all along. Jewish gangsters deliberately misled the Mafia into believing the intended victim was Mussolini in order to secure their help. When the news of the reward was announced one of Mancini's men must have decided to betray them for the money. With typical Mafia mentality he had not gone to the police but contacted Genovese instead. Probably he'd been told to accompany the three gunmen to the warehouse for identification purposes. Somehow the plot had failed — perhaps Siegel or his Italian accomplice had recognized one of the gunmen — and now all four of them were dead.

Bellini turned to Genovese and tried to extract more information from him.

"I will investigate what you have told me. In the meantime perhaps you would like to confirm the identities of the dead men. Only one of them was known to us."

Reluctantly Genovese gave him the names. Bellini then astonished Genovese by what he said next.

"I will investigate your information but I am not going to release his name or photograph to the public. If we are going to flush him out the last thing we need is publicity. A man who sees his picture posted all over Rome will go deeper into hiding. If I tell my superior officer he will have Siegel's face on every street corner so I will bide my time and wait till he reappears."

"I want that bastard dead! He's already killed five people since he arrived in Italy and there might be more if you don't stop him."

Bellini prepared to turn the screw.

"Four of the men he killed were Mafiosi. Three of them worked for you and one of your men was someone we've connected with a series of unsolved murders. If instead of sending those men to the warehouse to try to kill him you had reported the matter to me all of those men would probably still be alive."

"I thought because they knew Moretti it would be easier to lure them into a trap."

"You thought about the reward money and getting revenge on a rival gangster. You weren't interested in anything besides that. Until the very moment of the assassination you thought it was Mussolini who was in danger and yet you did not alert me to the presence of Siegel and his associate. Only after Hitler and your gunmen had been killed did you come to me. You withheld information that might have prevented the murder and for all your claimed friendship with Il Duce you were prepared to see him dead as long as you could lay your hands on the reward money."

Genovese took in the full implications of those deadly words. He realized Bellini had him in his power and that a single word from him could jeopardize his standing with the regime.

"I did not understand I was exposing Il Duce to such danger. I assumed — "

"Don't try and deceive me. I know exactly why you did nothing. Unless you have any further information for me I think that concludes our conversation, Signor Genovese. Do you have anything to add?"

Genovese shook his head and Bellini made a thoroughly welcome escape. He returned to his office and pondered his best course of action.

He began to consider what use he should make of this new information. Genovese clearly expected him to put out an immediate all points alert for the two men and inform his superior officer of the news. It would not be easy to track down the assassins but on the other hand it was going to be hard for them to get out of the country without Mafia assistance. Even two men as desperate as Siegel and his accomplice would be unable to evade the road blocks, the massive police and military presence and the absence of any means of support for them. It was not obvious how they could remain hidden for long and still less clear how they could make their escape.

As he considered all these factors Bellini relaxed slightly. Sooner or later the two fish would swim into his net and he would haul them safely into shore. The only real question was whether or not he should tell Captain Solanio what he now knew. In theory he had no choice but his conscience continued to trouble him.

Bellini tried to put himself into their shoes and imagine where they would go after escaping from the warehouse. They would be on foot so their progress would be slow. He decided to visit the area once more and investigate possible departure points. This time he went alone, using his own car rather than a police vehicle and driver. *He still had doubts about the right moral course of action. From the strictly legal point of view his duty was clear. He had to report Genovese's information to his superior officer and issue an immediate description of Siegel to the media.*

It was not that he felt any kind of admiration for the two assassins. Both men were presumably professional criminals who had almost certainly murdered other gangsters in the past. On the other hand it was difficult to feel the slightest sympathy for the victim.

Bellini pushed these troubling thoughts away as he parked his car at the warehouse and surveyed the immediate area. There were no houses in the vicinity but a little further on lay a church that stood on the edge of a suburban development with a patch of wasteland still awaiting further building. He entered the church and looked around for the priest. An elderly cleric appeared and Bellini introduced himself.

"Father, I am Lieutenant Bellini of the Carabinieri. I would like to ask you some questions. Were there any visitors to your church yesterday afternoon?"

"Yes, we have many visitors here. Local people come to pray but we also have tourists who come to admire the frescoes and our Caravaggio."

Bellini was not certain how much information the priest could give him but he pressed him to describe all the tourists he had seen in the church yesterday. None sounded remotely like Siegel or his accomplice so he appeared to have exhausted that line of enquiry. Thanking the priest he made his way outside and tried to determine the most likely direction in which the assassins might have travelled.

He began by exploring the surrounding area and saw three minor roads each of which he explored in turn. The first road led to a series of small villas and he did not bother to investigate that location. It led nowhere that would be useful to two foreign gangsters and he dismissed it without further consideration.

The second road led quickly on to a major highway. That was a far more likely route for the assassins to choose. If they had made their way on to that road they might have been able to take a taxi or even hitch-hike back into the centre of the city where there would be many possible hiding places particularly for two Mafiosi.

The third road led to the left bank of the Tiber. That seemed a more likely choice of exit and with a sudden realization he saw the inner logic of what he now imagined must be the path they had followed.

On the left bank of the Tiber lay Trastavere, the Jewish quarter of Rome. It seemed not only possible but probable that two Jewish gangsters who had just killed Hitler might have thought that the safest and most welcoming part of the city. Gunning the car, he returned to his office, deciding to investigate all known criminals with connections to the Trastavere district.

32

Bellini telephoned the woman whose apartment had been commandeered by the two assassins.

"Signora, this is Lieutenant Bellini of the carabinieri. I am sorry to trouble you but I would like to ask you one further question if I may. You said that one of the men who held you prisoner was Italian. Did he have a strong accent?"

The woman thought for a moment.

"Yes, he did have a Roman way of speaking. I thought he had that strange Trastaverini accent."

Bellini thanked her and was more convinced than ever that Trastavere was the key. The Trastaverini were known for their distinctive local accent and other Romans often mocked them when they came across it. Yes, he was sure that Siegel's accomplice came from that part of Rome and that the two of them were probably hiding out there at that very moment.

Trastavere was as astonished as any other part of Rome at the assassination of Hitler but because of the large Jewish population in the area few residents regretted his passing. Their only concern was that it might lead to some kind of reprisals against their own community. Bellini felt sure that here if anywhere in Rome the two men might have found refuge and even welcome for their deed.

He drove his car across the Tiber and entered Trastavere. He saw the people on the streets eying the presence of a stranger when he parked his car and stepped out on to the pavement. Immediately a small group of street urchins surrounded him. He knew what they wanted and resigned himself to the inevitable consequences of visiting the area unofficially rather than flanked by a group of squad cars.

"Hey, signor, want anything?" the oldest boy asked him.

He regarded the ragamuffin without enthusiasm and then pointed to his vehicle.

"Guard my car. See it's not stolen, broken into or vandalized. I'll make it worth your while."

He entered the maze of narrow lanes that lay at the heart of Trastavere. The air of poverty and neglect clung to every aspect of the area. He felt sad to think that in the great city where he lived so many of his fellow citizens endured such squalid conditions.

This is Rome, but a private Rome, one that the tourists never see. It's different in so many ways from the city I know. Most of the people here look on the police as their enemy rather than as guardians of law and order. How can I hope to pierce the hidden heart of a world so different from the Rome I know? What chance do I have of tracking down two killers if they've taken refuge in this isle of rejection of all the rest of Rome stands for?

He recognized an old adversary whom he had arrested a few years ago. Since the time of his arrest he had become an occasional informant for Bellini. Moving slowly and discreetly towards the man he tapped him softly on the shoulder.

"Luca Donato," he said quietly. "I would like to have a few words with you in private."

The man wheeled round at once and Bellini saw the glint of a knife in his hand. Even in Trastavere the criminals distrusted one another. He recognized Bellini at once and looked away shiftily.

"What do you want with me? I haven't done anything."

"It's not you I'm interested in. Have any new people come into the area over the last couple of days?"

"Why don't you just tell me what you want and I'll see if I can help you? All this talk is making me nervous as hell."

"All right. I believe that the men who assassinated Hitler may be hiding out in Trastavere."

Donato whistled when he heard that.

"I might have some information for you. It isn't much, but I suppose it might be of some value."

"What is it?" asked Bellini, instantly alert.

"Well, some of the neighbours round here say they heard a truck leaving round about 1.00 in the morning and coming back about 3.00. This was about two days before the assassination."

Bellini took in the information.

"I'll check it out. Take me to the house where this took place."

"It's not far away as it happens. Just over there in fact."

Donato pointed to Fredo's garage.

"Like I say, it might be nothing but you never know. Oh, and by the way, Fredo — that's the old Jew who lives above — was seen the next day carrying bags of shopping which is unusual for him as he lives on his own and only shops for essentials daily."

Bellini slipped some lire into Donato's hand. He walked across to Fredo's house and banged on the door. Fredo shuffled down the stairs and was astonished to see an unfamiliar visitor who was certainly not a Trastaverini.

"Can I help you?" he asked in a wheezing voice.

"I am Lieutenant Bellini of the Rome police. I need to ask you a few questions. May I come in?"

Fredo was overcome with an overwhelming sense of fear. In all the years he had lived in Trastavere he could not remember a policeman knocking on his door. *It must be because of Luigi and Benny. I will have to try and protect my nephew at all costs.*

"Please come in," he said, leading him up the stairs into to the living room.

Once they were inside he asked Bellini to sit down in an armchair while he poured himself a glass of water. As he did so he stumbled and the policeman immediately stood up and caught his arm before he fell.

"Sit down, please. I thought you were going to pass out."

"I haven't been well lately," Fredo said in a weak voice.

He nodded and waited for the old man to recover before continuing. He hated having to question someone like him rather than the normal suspects who passed in and out of the cells like a revolving door but he had no choice. When he was sure that Fredo had recovered he began questioning him about his movements.

"I have received reports that you drove your truck at about 1.00 in the morning and did not return until two hours later. That would be four nights ago. What were you doing and where were you going at that time of night?"

Fredo was under intense pressure and knew that he had to think quickly and somehow come up with an explanation that might satisfy this curious policeman.

"Four nights ago? Let me think for a moment. Oh yes, I remember now. I couldn't sleep that night. I could hardly breathe because it was such a muggy night. So I decided to do some night fishing for carp in the Tiber. It's my hobby; it helps me relax."

"Did anyone see you there?"

"I don't think so."

"You were observed buying more food than usual the following morning? Why was that?"

"Well, like I told you, I haven't been feeling very well so I thought I'd buy more before I got worse. I'm on my own, you know; I don't have anyone to look after me since my wife died."

"So you haven't had any visitors recently?"

"I'm afraid that visitors are a rare event, Lieutenant. I only wish I did have more of them."

Bellini glanced around the shabby room and his eyes fell upon a framed photograph.

"Who's that?"

"That's my nephew Luigi," Fredo said enthusiastically.

The moment he had uttered the name he regretted it. Bellini felt sorry for the old man but he immediately recognized the name Luigi. The coincidence of names and the connection with Trastavere struck him as too remarkable to be accidental. He picked up the photograph and studied it carefully.

"May I take this, please? I'll return it to you in a few days."

Fredo became distressed as he sensed that the policeman suspected something and it was his own fault for revealing his nephew's name and identity but he could hardly refuse without attracting suspicion.

"Have you seen him recently?"

"The last time I saw him was fourteen years ago. He emigrated to America. Of course he's done well over there. Much better than he would have done if he'd stayed here."

"I'm sure he has. I need to take a look at your truck."

Fredo ushered him through the internal staircase into the garage. Bellini examined the truck carefully and noticed a fishing rod lying against the wall.

"Did you catch any fish when you went to the Tiber?"

"I'm afraid not."

"Perhaps you'll be more fortunate next time."

The two men parted and Fredo immediately poured himself a stiff brandy to fortify his nerves after the ordeal he had just undergone. *Oh, Luigi, take care. May God go with you and protect you.*

Bellini walked back through the narrow streets until he reached his car. The street urchins were still standing in front of it and as far as he could see nothing was missing or damaged. Reluctantly he fished out some lire from his pocket and handed them over before driving off.

33

A warm glow of contentment came over Siegel and Carmona after they had finished eating. The dreadful events of that day were over. They would remain etched in their minds for ever but at least the immediate horror was behind them. Both men were relaxed and resumed their normal confident manner. Coffee was served in the lounge and Siegel sat next to Marianne on the sofa.

Upon retiring he spoke to Carmona.

"That Marianne's a real doll! Do you think she likes me?"

"Those two women could be our tickets to freedom. If you make a move on the girl it could screw everything up. We can't take the risk."

Reluctantly Siegel agreed.

Morning came to the villa where four people sat at the breakfast table. Celia and Marianne greeted them with a pot of hot coffee.

"Marianne and I have been talking things over. I don't know what your plans are but we're both returning to America on the *Conte di Savoia* tomorrow. Since we've both enjoyed your company so much I wonder if you'd care to join us on the voyage home."

Siegel's eyes lit up. It was the perfect solution to organizing their getaway.

"That's a wonderful offer. I've enjoyed your company so much and going back home together we could have a great time.'

"I have contacts with the shipping line. There won't be any difficulty about acquiring two extra tickets for you as the ship is usually only about half-full. Of course I understand that you may have other plans but if you're agreeable to my suggestion I'll go out now and get the tickets for you. Marianne and I will go into Rome and bring them back. You two can wait here till we return. And don't worry about the money; you can reimburse us when you get back to America."

Siegel was suspicious when she said that. *Why did the two women want to go into Rome and leave them behind? Was it a trap and were they heading off to alert the police? Had something he'd said or done given him away?*

"I'm not so sure. Luigi, let's talk it over. We need to be certain about our schedule."

Carmona moved quickly to try and defuse the situation.

The two men retreated hastily into the bedroom and Siegel immediately began voicing his suspicions.

"Something's not right. Why would they want to leave us and go into Rome on their own? I figure that Celia's on to us and she's going to rat us out to the cops!"

Carmona tried to reassure him but when Siegel was in a state of heightened suspicion he was a difficult man to control.

"If they wanted to get the cops on to us why not just ring them? Or slip out unnoticed during the night when we were asleep? Do you think we'll get a better chance of making it back home? Let's just be grateful for the gift they're offering."

Siegel considered what he'd just said. As he turned his words over in his mind another aspect of things struck him.

"You remember Trastavere?"

"Yes, of course. What about it?"

"You remember you told Fredo we were working for U.S. intelligence?"

"Yes, I remember."

"Well, I mean, are you? Are you really one of Uncle Sam's boys and I've just been hauled along for the ride? And are the two of them planning to rat me out to the authorities? Am I just the fall guy that you're going to let take the rap?"

"For Christ's sake, he's my uncle. I had to come up with some kind of story for him. I figured he'd find it a lot easier to accept his nephew working for intelligence than he would thinking he's a member of the Mafia. Do you remember where we met? And who was with us? Do you think Meyer Lansky and Frank Costello are working for Uncle Sam? Any more than Mancini is? Get a grip on yourself. I work for the Syndicate same as you."

His words had an effect on Siegel. *Yes, he might be working for the Feds but there's no way Meyer and Frank would set me up for some government hit. Maybe he is who he says.*

"I guess you're right. This whole business has been so weird from start to finish I'm starting to doubt everything and everyone. But I still don't like the idea of the two dames going into Rome on their own and leaving us behind. I'm going to make a suggestion of my own about that."

"What suggestion?"

Siegel did not bother to answer as he swept out of the bedroom and into the kitchen once more. Carmona followed him in with a growing sense of unease.

"Well, ladies, you've made us a very kind offer and we'd like to take you up on it. But we couldn't dream of letting you go into Rome on your own. We'll come with you."

Carmona managed to control the alarm on his face but Celia, who rarely displayed emotion, coughed suddenly to disguise her astonishment. Of course it was completely impossible to agree to his suggestion. The police might know about his part in the assassination by now and in any case she needed to meet her contact.

"That won't be necessary. We can organize a couple of tickets on our own. And I thought we might combine it with a shopping trip which would be very boring for the two of you."

Celia was flustered and although she was too experienced to show that to anyone who did not know her Marianne grasped the true nature of the situation immediately. She understood that Siegel was nervous, even paranoid, after what he'd been through and that his immediate assumption was that the two women were planning to turn him and Carmona over to the police. Before Celia got herself deeper into difficulties Marianne took charge of the situation.

"No, you go on your own, Aunt Celia. I don't much feel like going into Rome today. I'd rather stay here with Benny and have some fun!"

"Well, if you're quite sure."

"I'm sure. And I do hope Benny won't mind spending a few hours here with me."

Siegel relaxed completely when he heard that suggestion. There was no way Celia would betray them now with Marianne as a hostage. And with the older woman out of the way who knew what interesting and pleasant diversions might lie ahead?

"I'd like that very much," he said.

Celia still had misgivings about the idea but she realized that Marianne was shrewder than she'd thought and was able to improvise a plan in a crisis. Carmona would be with them so there was no reason to worry. He would control Siegel if he tried it on with Marianne. So far the plan seemed to be working to perfection and the younger woman had surpassed her expectations by extricating her from a potentially difficult situation.

34

Under the Nazis people had learned to be silent or at least to whisper in corners. Former friends found that suddenly people they had known for years were not at home when they called. Fear hung over the land like an invisible fog, strangling all that was best about the nation.

Not everyone in Germany was dismayed by the news of Hitler's death. The growing threat of war over the Sudetenland in Czechoslovakia had alarmed many people including a number of senior army officers.

General Ludwig Beck, Chief of the army general staff, felt the oppressive pall of terror more clearly than many. He had survived the Great War, revolution, civil war, economic disaster and the breakdown of democracy. At first he welcomed the Nazis as bringers of order, rebuilders of the economy, strong rulers who had restored the nation's pride.

For the first few years of Hitler's rule Beck continued to think positively of Hitler and the Nazis before, slowly and not with any sudden moment of illumination, the scales fell from his eyes. He once believed that Hitler was a great man surrounded by bad advisors. By 1938, it dawned on him that Hitler was the source of Germany's problems and that National Socialism was a philosophy of evil.

Now he is dead at last we have a chance to put right the damage, he thought. We can create a fairer nation without concentration camps and the Gestapo. Only the army can overthrow the Nazis and Hitler's assassination has given us the opportunity. The danger of war over the Sudetenland had alarmed him so much that he had consulted with like-minded people and made preparations for a military coup in the event of war.

Now Hitler was dead, and Beck digested the news and considered its consequences. He realized that Hess and Goering were the most likely successors with Goebbels and Himmler also candidates for the leadership. Messages of condolence began pouring in from across the world. The official reaction of every nation was to "regret" the assassination of Hitler.

Is a coup still necessary in the changed situation? I think so but will my fellow officers? Many of them simply fear the prospect of another war and do not see that the whole Nazi regime is evil and must be destroyed. With Hitler gone, will they still back me if I act?

Goering is as much of a warmonger as Hitler and if he takes over the country will still be in danger. Hess and Himmler and Goebbels might be less militaristic but they are all lunatics and who knows what they might do?

The cold wind of fear swept across him as he contemplated the consequences of failure. He and his fellow-conspirators would be dead and the Nazis stronger. The prize if he could succeed was an end to the whole National Socialist experiment and a return to sanity for his country.

Beck gazed out of the window of his office and hesitated. Should he strike a blow and risk everything or remain quiet and take no action? Beck observed the round-up of political opponents with increasing disquiet.

He knew at once that Goering and Heydrich were planning to strengthen the Nazi hold on power and if he did not act soon the opportunity would be lost.

His heart fluttered as he picked up the phone and began issuing orders. Leaving his office, Beck gathered together a small but loyal band of troops and made his way to the Reichs Chancellery.

35

Goering, his chest bedecked with medals as usual, was preening himself when Beck arrived at the Chancellery. He was preparing the text of his address to the nation and did not welcome the interruption.

"Well, general, what is it you want?"

"Reichsmarshal, now that the Führer has been so tragically slain the future of Germany is at stake."

"Yes, it is. And as the new leader of Germany I shall carry forward the legacy of National Socialism and fulfil the wishes of our Führer. There can be no turning back from the path of greatness upon which our nation has embarked. We will pursue with relentless vigor the Fuehrer's vision of a thousand-year Reich with borders stretching from the Urals to the Pyrenees."

Beck gazed thoughtfully into the face of the man sitting at his desk. In Goering's cold eyes he saw the glint of madness. All his doubts and fears, all his irresolution and hesitation, were swept away as he recognized a Goering-led Reich would be as dangerous and unpredictable as one led by Hitler.

Bowing and clicking his heels, Beck made his move. He reached for his pistol and pointed it straight into the face of the man sitting opposite.

"Reichsmarshal Goering, you are under arrest," he said quietly. "The army is taking temporary charge of the country in the new situation. For the moment I am the new leader of Germany."

Goering stared at Beck in disbelief. He had no inkling of any dissatisfaction among the military, and generals such as Keitel and Reichenau were fervent supporters of National Socialism and admirers of Hitler.

"What? This is treason, Beck! If you shoot me loyal troops will avenge my murder and you will hang like the traitor you are."

"There are soldiers outside who will follow my orders, Reichsmarshal. You may come with me as my prisoner or I will shoot you now or have my men shoot you while attempting to escape."

"You swore an oath of loyalty."

"Yes, I did. But that was to the Führer. Now he is gone I am released from my oath. Shall we go now? Or would you rather be shot?"

Goering gave him a look of utter contempt. He was no coward and momentarily he considered calling Beck's bluff and daring him to shoot. Reflecting more soberly, he wondered how much support Beck actually had within the army and whether or not he could maintain himself in power. Heydrich, as far as he knew, was still at large and could call on the resources of the SS, Gestapo and SA to form the nucleus of a counter-coup. Hess, Himmler, Goebbels and Keitel were still in Italy and therefore beyond Beck's reach at present. They would certainly not accept a military dictatorship and would work to overthrow it. All in all, perhaps temporary acquiescence in the situation was the wiser option.

"Where are you taking me?" he asked finally.

Beck felt a sense of relief as he knew that his most dangerous enemy had capitulated.

"To a place of safety, Reichsmarshal. No harm will come to you if you go quietly and if you co-operate with the new government."

Goering and Beck left the office to walk towards a waiting truck. Lines of Reichswehr soldiers with rifles made Goering realize he had no choice. The two men disappeared while Beck urgently considered the next phase of his plan.

36

General Beck knew the most obvious and immediate danger to the coup was the fact that Heydrich was still at large with the SS and Gestapo under his control. The SA would also be likely to follow Heydrich's orders rather than his own. He did not relish the prospect of taking on the well-armed and fanatical Nazi paramilitary units and he knew they would fight hard if they suspected the truth. There would be considerable bloodshed which would destabilize his coup and make it harder to maintain himself in power. It was essential to find and arrest Heydrich before a bloody confrontation occurred.

Heydrich had no idea that a coup had taken place. When he saw soldiers on the streets he assumed that they were there on Goering's orders and were as much a part of the plan to maintain order as his own mass arrests of dissidents.

One name that was high on Heydrich's list of people to arrest was Carl Goerdeler, the mayor of Berlin. For the last five years Goerdeler had criticized almost every aspect of Nazi rule, particularly the concentration camps and anti-Semitism. He had been arrested before but released. This time he would not be so fortunate.

Heydrich's busy cull of political opponents made him highly visible on the streets of Berlin. Before long his location had been reported to Beck by one of his trusted officers and the general knew he had to act quickly.

It was essential that the dangerous young man should suspect nothing. Beck decided to meet Heydrich directly and try to lure him into a trap. He left his office and went out on patrol with a number of troops and came upon his quarry at last.

"Herr Heydrich."

"General Beck."

Beck considered his options. The Deputy Leader of the SS had a group of a hundred armed men with him and he dared not risk an open confrontation on the street. Only guile would serve him now and he knew that if he could get Heydrich into custody his most pressing danger would be at an end.

"Reichsmarshal Goering asked for the three of us to meet at the Reichs Chancellery to co-ordinate our actions in the new situation," he said finally. "He has received word of a possible uprising by the Communists now that the Führer is sadly no longer able to guide us. The army, the SS and police will work together to neutralize that threat. If you would please accompany me to the Chancellery the three of us can prevent such a disaster from happening."

Heydrich turned to the men under his command and issued his orders.

"Carry on rounding up all known dissidents," he said. "Remember — our country's future is at stake."

He allowed Beck to lead him into his staff car where he was driven away to the Chancellery. As soon as they had reached the line of soldiers guarding the building Beck made his move. Drawing his gun he pointed it at his target's head.

"You are under arrest. If you attempt to resist you will be shot. You will be taken into protective custody until you are brought to trial. Long live Germany!"

Heydrich stared at Beck whose face remained impassive. He realized at once that the general was in the process of carrying out a coup d'état and considered his position. Hess, Himmler, Goebbels and Keitel were all in Italy. He and Goering represented the only serious challenge to Beck within Germany.

"Where is Reichsmarshal Goering?"

"Like you he is now in protective custody."

"You realize that the SS and SA are out in force?"

"Of course. But with both you and Herr Himmler out of the picture I doubt if they would act against the new government. Please accompany me to your new quarters."

Another wave of relief swept over Beck now that the dangerous Heydrich was safely under lock and key. He began issuing orders for the SS and SA to return to barracks and over the course of the next few hours they did so. The ordinary police force also arrested a number of people that Beck had identified as dangerous and by late afternoon he felt confident enough in the success of the coup to approach various people with a view to forming a new, non-Nazi government.

In Berlin, acting on Beck's orders, troops from the 23rd Infantry Division were busy occupying all the key government ministries. They also took possession of the radio stations and the police, Gestapo and SS facilities in Berlin. All the telephone exchanges were captured and the city was effectively sealed off from the rest of Germany. His soldiers also took control of Tempelhof Airport and soon Berlin was securely in the hands of the plotters. The next step was to extend the control of the army over the whole country.

Beck issued orders to other army commands throughout Germany. He still had to deal with the impending return of Hess, Himmler, Goebbels and Ribbentrop and was particularly nervous about Keitel. He was a strong Nazi sympathizer and Hitler had recently spoken of promoting him to Field Marshal. He would certainly do everything in his power to reverse the coup.

37

The speed of the take-over worked in Beck's favor but it would not be long before news penetrated abroad. Knowing that boldness was his only course of action, he telephoned Rome. After a few minutes delay he was put through to Hess.

"Herr Hess, the nation is in mourning for the sad loss of our Führer. In the changed circumstances it would be best if you, Herr Goebbels, Herr Himmler, Herr Ribbentrop, Herr Keitel and Herr Raeder flew back to Berlin at the earliest possible moment."

"Where is Goering? I tried to ring him earlier but was told he was unavailable."

"Herr Goering is busy maintaining order in the new situation. So too," he anticipated the next question, "are Herr Heydrich and Herr Bormann. I am in temporary charge and we need our nation's leaders to return home immediately."

"We could fly back to Berlin with the Führer's body and leave the rest of the party to make their way home on the train. Is the Gestapo investigating the assassination?"

"Of course. Numerous suspects have already been placed in custody."

"Good. We will fly out this evening."

"I shall await your safe return."

Beck reflected as he put down the phone that he now had Goering, Heydrich, Bormann, Rosenberg, Speer and

Ley in custody. All the senior Nazi leaders were in Rome and preparing to return home. The coup appeared to have been a complete surprise and to date there had been no opposition or bloodshed. *This could be a new dawn for our country, Beck thought, an end to the mindless thuggery of National Socialism. I can feel proud once more of being a German.*

38

Celia took the car and drove into Rome. Although she had not made a specific assignation with her superior officer she knew that he went to a particular cafe between ten thirty in the morning until around midday and that the place was always somewhere they could meet if they needed to make a rendezvous.

"Good morning, Bill. We need to talk."

They made their way through the still deserted streets.

"Everything on schedule?"

"It is now. There was a possible problem this morning but Marianne improvised brilliantly and got us out of it. Both men will be sailing on the *Conte di Savoia* tomorrow."

"Glad to hear it. Anything you need from me or is everything prepared?"

"I'd say we were completely on top of the situation but there's an outside chance that there could be a difficulty. You know Genovese, of course."

"Sure. What of it?"

"Siegel killed three of his men yesterday as well as one of Mancini's men who'd turned informer hoping for a share of the reward. If Genovese goes to the police there could be a problem getting them on to the ship."

"Who's the officer in charge of the case?"

"Lieutenant Bellini."

"I know the guy you mean. I'll see how the land lies and if I have to I'll see what strings I can pull."

"Anything else we need to do?"

"You need to organize a cab for tomorrow morning and be on the tourist bus taking you to the port. Once you land in New York we can relax and forget any of this ever happened."

"I can't wait."

39

The three of them waited anxiously for Celia to return from her assignation in Rome. Siegel moved across to the radio and turned it on. He asked Carmona to interpret if there were any news bulletins but at the moment only light music was playing on the station.

When the music on the radio came to an end the regular news bulletin began. Five minutes of news followed, most of it dominated by the assassination of Hitler and its aftermath. Carmona listened intently and finally gave a brief summary of the news.

"In the first place they're still trying to find out who killed Hitler. The German delegation is leaving Italy today and going back home on the train. Four bodies have been found in an industrial estate on the outskirts of Rome and the police think that the dead men were shot in a Mafia killing. Il Duce has ordered a day of mourning and the German government has declared a week of national mourning."

Marianne's eyes widened in horror as she pretended to hear the news about the Mafia killings for the first time.

"Four men shot dead on top of Hitler's assassination? That's an awful thing to happen! I'm beginning to wonder how safe Italy really is. Maybe it's a good thing we're going back home tomorrow."

Then the front door opened.

"Celia's back," Marianne shouted.

The three of them got up and rushed towards the entrance hall. Celia removed her felt green hat and took off her green gloves before laying them on the hall table. They saw the satisfied expression on her face and sensed that she had succeeded in purchasing two more tickets for the sailing. She opened her handbag and waved the tickets in the air with a gesture of triumph.

"Didn't I tell you I had influence? I've purchased two second-class tickets for the *Conte di Savoia* leaving Rome at noon tomorrow."

Marianne jumped for joy and Siegel, to her astonishment, hugged Celia. He had to hold back his tears as he spoke to her.

"God, I love you both!"

Celia stared at him in disbelief and even Marianne looked surprised. He was overwhelmed with joy at the realization that he was soon going to be leaving Italy and at last it seemed that they had a workable plan.

Celia gave both men their passports and tickets.

"Now we need to start thinking about packing and getting back home again," she said.

"Come upstairs and I'll help you pack," said Marianne excitedly, taking Siegel by the hand and leading him into the bedroom.

She pulled out two suitcases from under the bed and placed them on top. She pointed to the wardrobe.

"You can pack any clothes you want. The owner won't mind and anyway you can get yourself a whole new outfit on the ship!"

After the packing was completed they went into the kitchen and set about the task of cleaning and polishing their shoes. They switched on the radio where a Cole Porter song was playing and all of them sang happily along with the music.

"This is our song," Siegel said as he looked at Marianne. "You're the tops, you're the Coliseum!"

Siegel grabbed her and they danced to the music for a few minutes before the song ended and Celia broke the spell again.

"We need to start preparing the evening meal," she told Marianne. "We'll eat in about an hour."

The two men settled down and waited for the meal. Both of them tried to focus on the following day when they hoped to be out of Italy at last and sailing for America and safety.

"It won't be long before we can leave," said Carmona.

"It can't come soon enough for me."

40

Hess and his fellow-leaders flew into Tempelhof airport at Berlin. They still mourned the death of the Führer and the presence of his coffin on the plane was a constant reminder of their loss. It was draped in black and with both the flag of Imperial Germany and of the Third Reich covering the coffin.

Searchlights greeted the arrival of their aircraft and there were a number of armed soldiers waiting to meet them. As they stepped off the plane they gave the Hitler salute which the leaders returned.

"The Führer's body is in our plane," Hess told them. "We must give him the funeral such a great man deserves."

There was no hint of anything unusual about their reception. The soldiers were quiet and respectful and they passed into the main terminal without incident.

When they walked on towards the exit they recognized the familiar face of General Beck waiting. He had a number of soldiers with him but again this raised no alarm bells. Hitler had just been assassinated and perhaps they would be the next targets.

"Gentlemen," said Beck, saluting. "I understand that you have the body of our Führer in the plane."

"Yes, we do," Hess said. "Our whole nation must be in mourning for his passing."

"Yes, it is. In the meantime please come outside. We have arranged transport for you."

He took Hess, Goebbels, Himmler and Ribbentrop towards the exit, gesturing to General Keitel and Admiral Raeder to remain behind. As they left the airport building and walked into the open air they saw a thousand soldiers facing them. Beck made his way outside, knowing that the hour of decision had come at last. Turning to his troops, he gave the signal for them to present arms.

"Gentlemen," he said, looking at the Nazi leaders, "you are under arrest. Long live Germany!"

Hess stared at Beck, frozen into immobility and silence. Himmler gazed around the scene, carefully weighing up the odds. Ribbentrop's mouth gaped open in stunned disbelief. Only Goebbels showed spirit and defiance in the face of these unexpected developments.

"This is treason! We are the government of Germany, not you. Who put you up to this? You are a traitor, Beck, and you will die a traitor's death!"

"I can shoot you now or I can have you arrested and put on trial. The choice is yours."

Goebbels looked at Himmler who remained silent. Hess and Ribbentrop appeared incapable of decision and he either had to risk being cut down in a hail of bullets or accept being arrested and hope to fight another day.

Reluctantly he fell silent and allowed himself and his colleagues to be led away. By the end of that day all the senior Nazi leaders were under arrest and many lower ranking ones too. The SA and SS had been rounded up and many of their members were in custody.

One of Beck's aides ushered away Raeder, the head of the navy. Another soldier took Keitel away. Once the Nazi leaders were safely on the truck taking them into custody, Beck returned to face them.

"We have a new situation in Germany following the assassination of the Führer," he told them. "The army has taken temporary charge of the country in the interests of national unity. As I am afraid that I cannot be sure of your loyalty I must place you both under immediate arrest."

Keitel stared at Beck with a look of astonishment.

"This is a military coup. The Nazi Party represents the legitimate government of the nation and I refuse to recognize your authority. I demand that you surrender to me immediately."

Beck produced a pistol and pointed it at Keitel's head.

"Do you want me to shoot you? It would be easy to place the gun in your hand after you are dead and report that you committed suicide."

Keitel looked at Raeder who was silent. Clearly Beck would shoot and then there would be no chance of organizing a counter-coup.

"If I go with you what is to stop me calling out to the soldiers that you are a traitor and that they should shoot you immediately?"

"Nothing prevents you from saying that. But it would do you no good. All the men you see out there have been hand-picked for this operation. They follow my orders and not yours."

Keitel gazed at him, contempt burning in his eyes.

"You have betrayed the honour of the officer corps, the army and the whole nation. This coup of yours will not survive, Beck. The nation is committed to National Socialism and you will be overthrown and executed."

"You may be right. But in the meantime you are my prisoners. I will escort you to a place of safe-keeping."

Reluctantly the two men followed Beck out of the room and into captivity.

Beck felt an overwhelming sense of relief that the coup had been bloodless — at least so far.

41

Dawn broke over the skies of Rome. It was still quiet with only the sound of songbirds in the oak trees disturbing the silence. All four of them were ready and sitting quietly at the villa waiting for the imminent arrival of the taxi. Siegel was nervous and even the rest of the party felt a growing tension as the possibility of their eventual return home came closer. All of them tried to put on a cheerful front as if they really were nothing more than holidaymakers looking forward to going back to America at last.

Each member of the party was lost in their own thoughts with Siegel going over in his mind the sequence of events from his arrival in Italy to the moment when he had shot Genovese's gunmen and the traitor Moretti. *The high point of his journey was of course the assassination of Hitler. He would always remember vividly the scene of the brief moments when the two of them had fired with deadly accuracy and removed the Nazi leader from the face of the earth for good.*

Carmona was reflecting on the fact that when he returned to New York he would be able to bid a welcome farewell to Siegel and never see him again. He was the most difficult partner he had ever been forced to work with and he looked forward with a real sense of relief to less complicated assignments on his return to the service.

On the other hand he was grateful to him for saving his life.

All four of the party were aware that dangers still lay ahead. When the taxi finally arrived at 6.00 they loaded their suitcases into the trunk while Celia made a last minute check of the villa. Once she was satisfied that all evidence of their presence was gone she parked the car in the garage and locked it securely. Her last action was to lock the front door and join the rest of them in the back seat of the cab.

The taxi headed for the western perimeter of Rome where they would pick up the shuttle bus taking them to the port of Civitavecchia. They asked the driver to avoid driving through the centre of the city but to stick to the outlying roads. As they drove along the leafy highways they noticed groups of police and soldiers standing around or in their official vehicles. They observed their presence with a slight feeling of unease but nothing happened. Eventually the taxi arrived at their destination and dropped them off at the Hotel Lorenzo on the west side of Rome. They got out of the cab and paid the driver before standing outside the hotel with their suitcases ready to be loaded on to the shuttle bus. A cool breeze blew and freshened the muggy air as rays of sunlight slowly pierced the clouds.

Within twenty minutes of their arrival at the hotel the shuttle bus arrived. It would be a two-hour journey from the hotel to the port and they showed the driver their tickets for the ship and their passports before he took away their luggage and stowed it safely in the hold.

There were around thirty other fellow-passengers on the coach, all American and eager to get back home. Carmona sat beside Celia and Marianne next to Siegel. They listened to the passengers talking and not surprisingly the events of the last few days dominated their conversation.

An elderly woman was talking excitedly to her co-passenger.

"All my life I wanted to visit Rome. Now all I want to do is get back. If I never see the place again it'll be too soon! In the last two days we've had five brutal killings. All the sights are closed and the streets are crawling with police and armoured tanks. It's like being in a war zone. I may come from Chicago but I've never seen anything like this."

Siegel tried to restrain an almost irresistible desire to laugh when the woman turned around abruptly and stared straight at him.

"Did you like him?"

"Who, ma'am?"

"Hitler, of course."

"Certainly not, ma'am. He was nothing but a troublemaker."

"Well, I didn't like him either, but you don't kill a person just because you don't like them."

Marianne interrupted the conversation by offering a bag of sweets around. The passengers began to relax as the coach left the suburbs of Rome and entered the open countryside. They passed olive groves and vineyards and trees that shaded them during their passage. This was the main artery leading out of the city into the low hills of Lazio.

The motion of the coach made him feel drowsy and Siegel decided to close his eyes and try to grab some sleep. He had dozed off for around half an hour when a sharp shudder awoke him as the coach ground to a halt. He opened his eyes and tried to follow what was happening at the front of the coach. Through the driver's window he saw an endless queue of traffic that stretched out bumper to bumper. The company representative walked down the aisle of the coach trying to reassure the passengers but even his voice sounded tense and uncertain.

"I think it's a police road block," he said. "Everyone needs to get their passports and tickets ready for inspection by the police."

Both men stiffened in their seats when they heard the news. Siegel took out his passport and studied it intently. *Do I still look like the picture in my phoney passport? My hair's a bit longer but I've still got the moustache. I just hope they're not on to us and they're not looking for Benny Siegel. I must remember my new name — Benjamin Bradley.* His head was racing as he tried desperately to reassure himself that everything would be all right and it was probably only a routine stop. There was probably nothing to worry about but he had a long history of brushes with the law. He had also recently committed five killings on Italian soil so he was far more nervous than usual.

Taking out the ticket for the ship he studied it carefully, noting that it had today's date upon it and a sailing time of noon. *All I can do now is hope.*

The shuttle bus inched its way slowly towards the road block. Finally they arrived and the coach doors opened. Two members of the carabinieri stepped into the vehicle. Siegel's eyes fell on the pistols in their holsters as they walked from the front of the coach towards the rear.

As they drew near to where he was sitting Marianne grabbed Siegel's arm and snuggled into him with an open display of affection.

"Passports and tickets," the officer said in poor English but with an authoritative voice.

The policeman noticed Marianne and studied her with obvious interest. She smiled back at him coyly. They handed over their papers and the policeman opened Siegel's passport and asked him for his name.

"Benjamin Bradley," he answered, hoping his voice sounded calmer than he felt.

The carabinieri officer handed them back the passports and tickets and after a final glance at Marianne he grinned at Siegel.

Then he moved on to Carmona and Celia who were eating some olives and fruit from napkins on their lap. He quickly examined their papers and took almost no notice of the middle-aged couple.

When he'd moved away from them and passed further along the coach Siegel turned to Marianne.

"I think he assumes we must be lovers. You know what these Italians are like!"

The shipping line rep was become increasingly agitated as the search continued. He began running up and down the coach and shouted angrily at the officers in Italian. Siegel turned around to Carmona and asked what he was saying.

"He says that he's responsible for the passengers and it's his job to make sure we all get to the ship on time. The police have told him they'll check the hold and then we can move on."

It was another twenty minutes before the police had concluded their search of the coach's hold. The bus started up again and the engine purred as they drove off once more. Siegel and Carmona looked at each other with a deep sense of relief and then admired the landscape from the window of the coach as the journey towards the port continued.

Soon they reached the shimmering coastline and drove past resorts where families played on the sandy beaches. It was refreshing and deeply reassuring to see such signs of normality and life continuing even in the face of tragedy. Young girls were laughing happily, old women dressed in black shielded themselves against the sun with their parasols and virile young men displayed their tanned and toned bodies beneath the warm sunlight.

The road signs began to point towards Civitavecchia and the coach finally pulled up outside the Michelangelo Fortress marking the entrance to the port.

The passengers alighted from the coach and took their luggage with them as they formed an orderly queue through the security gates. Their tickets and passports were checked and then they entered a large hall where everyone's luggage was opened and examined. After that process had been completed it was removed and taken on board the ship to be left outside the passengers' staterooms.

The four of them cleared customs at last and walked in to the terminal building. There were still two hours before the ship was due to sail. They knew that they would be admitted on board an hour before sailing but there was still some time to go. All they could do now was wait.

42

Beck's early relief at the success of the coup had almost turned into complacency. Within two days he had confined the SS and SA to barracks, arrested all the senior Nazi leaders and neutralized the Gestapo. What he had not sufficiently considered were the practicalities of running the country.

When he appointed Carl Goerdeler as the new Chancellor and invited him to form a government things ran smoothly at first. The Social Democrat Julius Leber was persuaded to join and a fairly broad-based coalition of moderate socialists, liberals and conservatives joined Goerdeler's cabinet. Unfortunately a contentious issue immediately raised its head between the two leading members of the new coalition government.

"There must be new elections to the Reichstag," Leber said. "How else will our government enjoy any legitimacy?"

"Are you mad? If we held elections now the Nazis would win by a landslide."

"So what do you propose? An indefinite military dictatorship?"

"I'm not sure what to do. And of course Beck's arrested all the German Nazis. We can't just kill them and we daren't put them on trial. All we can do is keep them locked up and hope that somehow the situation stabilizes."

"So you haven't got a plan? Wonderful! Does Beck have any ideas?"

"If he has then he hasn't shared them with me. I suppose we'll have to rule under the Enabling legislation Hitler brought in. Ironic but it's the only card we can play right now."

"And of course we haven't got a President to legitimize rule by decree either. Unless Beck plans to raise himself to that office."

"It can only be a temporary measure, we know that."

"At least we agree on something. Sooner or later we'll have to hold new elections."

"And what if we do — and the Nazis win? Do you think Goering or Himmler or Hess will just let us go into opposition?"

"I know the dangers but at some point we must take the risk. What do we stand for if our rule is as arbitrary as the Nazis? All we can do is try and educate the people and hope they can see through Hitler's lies."

"I suppose we could try and persuade some more — moderate Nazis — to join with us in a government of national unity."

Leber laughed out loud at that suggestion.

"Moderate Nazis! Where do you plan to find them? For the last five years I've only come across one kind of Nazi. And why should they join a coalition rather than try to rule alone? That idea's a non-starter."

"What's your alternative? You're quick enough to criticize my suggestions. Do you have any of your own?"

"Only to allow freedom of expression and try to show the people an alternative to Hitler. Other than that I can't think of anything that might work."

The men around the table gazed at each other thoughtfully, stuck in an impasse and unable to see any credible way out. Then Leber spoke once more.

"Besides all the constitutional issues, there's are two pressing foreign policy matters that need to be discussed. One of course is the Sudetenland; I'm assuming that Beck doesn't want us to go to war over that issue but who knows? The other is the Spanish Civil War. Should we pull out our troops and the Luftwaffe and leave Mussolini to support Franco on his own? Or do we just carry on as before?"

"I assume you'd like us to withdraw."

"Of course I would. We should never have got involved in the first place. It's a waste of life and the war's getting increasingly brutal. I felt ashamed when we bombed Guernica."

43

The dissension among the new Cabinet was so intense that Goerdeler felt it necessary to contact Beck. At the news that his newly assembled team were finding it hard to agree on anything the general grew exasperated.

"If you're going to keep on squabbling like the Weimar politicians I might as well have let the Nazis carry on! What are the main problems?"

Goerdeler knew that the future of Germany was at stake and that somehow agreement had to be reached. On the issue of new elections Beck agreed with him.

"Of course we'll have to let the people vote at some point but we need at least a year — maybe even two — to undo the harm Hitler's done. He's brainwashed the people so much it will be hard for you to get them to accept a different message. Leber will have to wait."

"The other issue is also complex. Leber wants us to withdraw from Spain. We know Mussolini will continue supporting Franco but he doesn't want us to be involved."

Beck glared at Goerdeler when he heard that.

"We can't withdraw from Spain. It's a matter of honour. And the experience of actual combat flying has been invaluable to the Luftwaffe."

"So you're telling me our continuing presence in Spain is non-negotiable?"

"I don't see how we could honourably withdraw. Mussolini would be enraged and some of my fellow officers would regard it as deserting two allies. To say nothing of the encouragement it might give Stalin to step up Russian involvement. Do you want Spain to go Communist?"

"Of course not. But I don't want it to go fascist either. What about scaling down our level of military involvement? We wouldn't withdraw completely but we'd reduce the scale of our commitment and leave most of the fighting to the Italians."

"On what basis would you justify reducing our involvement? The economy's booming, Franco is slowly winning the war, Britain and France don't want to get involved. I don't see how we could possibly justify reducing our military commitment. Mussolini would certainly not be pleased."

"Mussolini again! What exactly are your plans for the future direction of German foreign policy? We know Hitler wanted to move east towards Russia and Czechoslovakia. We know some Nazis wanted to get back our colonies in Africa and Asia. What about you, General? Do you want Germany to expand or not? And are you willing to go to war?"

Beck stared at Goerdeler in surprise. The mayor had rarely been so explosive and he could see the logic of his question.

"Of course I don't want to go to war. We had enough of that last time round. All those senseless deaths and at the end of it our country was in revolution and civil war. Yes, I'd like the Sudetens to join up with us and I'd like to get Danzig and Alsace-Lorraine back. But not at the expense of war. As for colonies, they're not worth it. It costs more to run them than you get back in revenue."

The two men gazed into the distance, each trying to find a solution to a number of pressing problems but unable to arrive at any conclusion.

"You are the first non-Nazi Chancellor since Schleicher," Beck said. "Surely you can manage to resolve your differences?"

"Schleicher is hardly an encouraging precedent. Not only did he fail but Hitler murdered him."

"We will all be dead men if the Nazis get back into power. Whatever the cost we must act together to prevent that from happening."

"We could start by lifting censorship on the media and legalizing political parties and allowing them to campaign."

"Of course if you do that the Nazis will use the media to demand immediate elections. How will you respond to that?"

Goerdeler fell silent, contemplating the practical difficulties of trying to restore the nation's freedom after five years of Nazi rule.

"Perhaps you're right. We'd better keep a lid on things and promote our own ideals before we begin lifting the restrictions. It's not what any of us wants but it might be the only way to stop the Nazis getting back into power."

"I'm beginning to wonder why I thought a civilian government was worth having. It might be more straightforward with a military dictatorship."

Goerdeler raised an eyebrow at that.

"Well, if you don't want dissent you might as well have left the Nazis in charge. We both know it will be hard to restore normality to our country but that's what we both want. I'm asking you outright — if we take a collective Cabinet decision will you countermand it if you disagree with our policy?"

"I would prefer not to have to do that but I cannot entirely rule out the possibility."

"In that case, I formally tender my resignation as Chancellor. Unless I have full authority to take decisions there is no point in continuing the charade of a civilian government. If you see us only as a fig leaf to cover the reality of military rule I cannot serve my country on that basis."

Beck blinked at the unexpected obstinacy shown by Goerdeler. He had been chosen by the General as his candidate for Chancellor because he was conservative and nationalist but a relatively moderate example of both tendencies. He saw Goerdeler as a unifying candidate who would be able to bring together most non-Nazi and non-Communist strands of opinion. Now his plan for a grand coalition of moderates appeared to be unravelling.

"None of us can afford to fail," he said. "The Gestapo, the camps, the pogroms — all these things have made me feel ashamed to be a German. How can we give up now? Our nation has been plunged into darkness for five long years. We have a chance now to redeem the honour of our nation. It matters, Carl."

His use for the first time of the mayor's Christian name struck Goerdeler. It was a conscious attempt to woo him and make him reconsider his decision.

For a moment he contemplated his course of action. If he resigned there were not many politicians capable of holding together a coalition. No doubt the Nazi leaders, even in custody, were busy making plans and trying to rally support for a counter coup.

"I will see what I can do," Goerdeler answered. "But you must allow me to rule and you must let our Cabinet take our decisions independently. We're in enough trouble without fighting among ourselves."

The two men parted, each increasingly anxious about the future. Goerdeler's sombre mood was not improved when he returned to the Chancellery and was promptly handed a message by his personal assistant.

"Chancellor, President Benes of Czechoslovakia has been on the telephone. He wishes to speak with you about the Sudetenland."

"He'll have to wait. I'll discuss the whole issue with the Cabinet before I talk to him."

With everything else that's been going on I'd completely forgotten about the Sudeten question. The one thing we all agree on is that we don't want to go to war over it. I need to familiarize himself with Hitler's demands and see if some kind of compromise agreement can be reached.

44

The four of them waited in the port, all preparing to depart from Rome. Carmona carried some orange juice over to the women while Siegel stood outside smoking a cigarette. He could smell the sea and saw the departure piers and the *Conte di Savoia* already in dock after its arrival from Genoa. The ship was bathed in sunlight and glistened against the background of a turquoise sea. Siegel looked at the ship and knew that it represented freedom and a safe return to his home and family. He was momentarily mesmerized by the effect of the sunlight and waters upon the appearance of the vessel and felt a sudden inner tranquillity as he took in its imposing appearance. It was much more modern than the *Vulcania* and had been built in 1932. The ship's decorative appeal was considerable and it was considered to be an exceptionally beautiful vessel.

It stopped at Civitavecchia to pick up tourists from Rome before making a final stop at Naples before sailing on to its final destination of America. Siegel looked around and saw that most of the other passengers seemed to be quite stressed out and particularly families with young children. *God, no matter how hard they think their life is they can't possibly know what the last few days have been like for me! None of them has had to go through what me and Luigi did. Thank God it's all over now and we'll be back in the U.S.A. and things will go back to normal at last.*

The thought of home brought a feeling of contentment after the ordeal of the dangerous and taxing mission to kill Hitler. *Waves of relief flooded him as he looked forward to seeing his wife and daughters again. It had all been worth it and in just over a couple of weeks he'd be back home. He saw the lights of New York dancing before his eyes and the magical theatres of Broadway, the cinemas where Hollywood films provided escapism for the people, the bars, the restaurants, the rich flavour of life in a city where hustle and bustle were an everyday reality. He loved the excitement of New York, the city that never sleeps, the place where you could get anything and where you could really live your dreams to the full. Siegel passed into a reverie where the memory of his native city filled him with a sense of utter delight.*

The wailing of police sirens in the distance broke the spell of his enchanted dreams. It was clear that they were in the distance but he could tell by the increasing volume of the sirens that they were approaching ever closer to where he and Carmona were. To his horror he saw four police vans screeching to an abrupt halt outside the terminal building.

Christ, he thought, they've got us now. After all we've gone through and just when we figured we were home and dry the bastards are on to us. His heart pounded as he rushed back inside the building to speak urgently with Carmona.

Pulling him to one side, he explained that he had just seen a convoy of police arriving at the port. In spite of the low tone of his voice the agitation in it was unmistakable.

"They know we're here," said Siegel, his face flushed with his breathless exertions. "We're surrounded. It's curtains for us now for sure!

Carmona watched them carefully through the glass windows and saw the police in the process of spreading out around the perimeter of the embarkation bay. They were busy setting up a cordon that would make it impossible for them to get out of the port.

"What now?" Siegel asked. "We're just sitting ducks and we haven't even got our guns. What the hell can we do about it?"

At that moment an announcement came over the loudspeaker system.

"All passengers for the *Conte di Savoia* please make your way to pier three where the ship will soon be ready to depart."

45

Both men looked intently at each other. In different ways each was normally fearless. Now, their habitual barrier of self-assurance was fractured by the sense of immediate and possibly terminal danger. They had no illusions about what would happen to them if they were arrested by the Italian police. The two of them had come on this long journey and planned every detail of the execution and thought that they were finally safe. Now, at the last possible moment, it seemed as if all their hard work had been for nothing. They would either be shot dead on the tarmac or taken away to face execution. Neither man was sure what to do but eventually Carmona tried to reassure Siegel as best he could.

"We don't actually know they're looking for us. It might just be a routine port search or maybe they're hoping to scare somebody into doing something stupid. We'll just have to go out with the rest of the passengers and face our destiny whatever it is. I really thought we'd made it. Maybe now would be a good time to start praying for a miracle!"

"Maybe it would."

The two men went back to Marianne and Celia and told them to join the queue outside and told them that they would see them on the ship shortly but that they had some last minute things to take care of first. Both women moved into line while Siegel and Carmona walked away and stood at some distance before they finally saw the end of the queue. Joining it as it shuffled its way towards the ship, they felt as if they were already dead men walking, simply waiting for the inevitable moment of doom to descend upon them.

A black police car drew up as the two men stood in line on the tarmac outside the terminal. A few more short steps and they would be on the ship and free from fear, yet the imminent approach of the police had altered their expectations drastically. Were all their hopes of return nothing but idle dreams about to be smashed into a thousand pieces by the bullets of the carabinieri or the executioner's rope?

46

As the two men shuffled hesitantly towards the gangway, Bellini stepped out of the car and looked around at his officers, all armed and in position. Satisfied with their placement he stood there for a moment, a tall figure preparing to make his move. He was not ready to unleash his troops on the quarry.

Bellini scanned the faces of the passengers as they made their way along the gangway and into the vessel. Siegel and Carmona hoped and prayed that it was only an unfortunate coincidence. Had he really discovered their true identities and the true purpose of their visit to Italy?

Carmona recognized Bellini instantly as the Lieutenant who had been in charge of rounding up the Mafia members at the garment factory only a few days earlier. Bellini recognized Carmona from the photograph he had seen in Fredo's apartment and knew at once who he was. He also saw the unmistakable figure of Siegel whose face he had studied intently and committed to memory following his delving in the basement archives.

All three of them stood around irresolute. It was obvious that flight would be impossible.

As he continued looking at the rapidly dwindling line of passengers entering the ship Bellini was torn by the pull of conflicting emotions. He realized that he was in a sense deciding whether or not to play God. He was certain that if he went up to them and either arrested or shot them he would have brought the assassins to justice and resolved the most difficult case of his entire career to the satisfaction of everybody. Perhaps he would even win a promotion as a result. Failure to do so would mean that he had allowed two gangsters to get away with murder.

His head was whirling with a turbulent ocean of thoughts and doubts. Bellini knew that it was impossible for him to hesitate any longer. The hour of decision awaited and he knew that he either had to confront the two men directly or turn around again and let them go.

He had been debating his course of action for some time but that morning it had become more complicated than ever. An unexpected phone call to the station had lured him away to a rendezvous at a cafe where he met a middle-aged American man. What he told Bellini had shocked him and at first he had simply refused to believe the story.

It was only after Bill had provided him with a few dates, names and facts that corresponded exactly with the information Bellini had obtained and was not known to the general public that he began to understand that his story was true. The assassination of Hitler had been carried out by Benny Siegel and Luigi Carmona but the gangster had been used as a tool by the U.S. government and his companion worked for the FBI.

His head was reeling as he digested the information. How was he supposed to deal with the new situation? His first loyalty was to the Italian government and it was his duty to arrest or kill the assassins. Now this American agent was asking him to let the two men sail back to the

United States and to allow the murder of Hitler to remain an unsolved crime.

His professional conscience as a policeman made him feel shame at the very idea. He knew who the killers were and he knew they would soon be leaving from the port of Rome. How could he let them get away with murder? He had dedicated his life to upholding the law.

He made his decision. With a brisk walk in his step he began walking towards them until he could see them clearly. Even from a distance he thought that the taller man looked slightly like Siegel. As he came closer his certainty increased with every step he took.

The two men tried to look as inconspicuous as possible as they waited in the queue to be able to go on board the ship and to seem like any other passenger but both men knew that they had committed murder and that the chances were that the day of reckoning for their actions had come at last.

Bellini slowly made his way forward. When he got to within ten feet of them he stopped. *These are the two killers beyond a doubt.*

He stared at them with an utter intensity of focus. Siegel and Carmona could not take their eyes off him either. They stayed where they were and their feet were fastened into a position of immobility. Their eyes locked into his with the certain knowledge that they had failed.

Bellini's face was fixed and not the slightest sign of emotion showed upon it. In spite of his outward calm he was experiencing the most profound inner turmoil of his life.

Bellini pulled his jacket open to reveal the pistol in his holster.

"He thinks we're armed," said Carmona.

Siegel stared at the policeman and prepared to raise his hands in a gesture of surrender before Carmona touched his arm lightly but firmly to restrain him.

"No, wait."

All the energy and vitality had sapped out of Siegel's body and a sense almost of resignation came over him as he contemplated the approaching moment of his own death.

Both men thought of their loved ones and Siegel also remembered his own saying. "A tough guy is a man who believes in something enough to kill or be killed." Now he had to put the truth of his own proverb to the test.

As he stared back at Bellini a final look of defiance showed on his face.

47

Bellini felt his thoughts racing around in desperate confusion. He looked at the two men who stood before him, clearly nervous and resigned to their fate. These were the same two men who had assassinated Hitler, himself a tyrant who had killed thousands of other people. They had also killed four *Mafiosi* who had themselves murdered many other gangsters. The dead men had made their living from drugs, prostitution and extortion.

Siegel and Carmona had not killed innocent people, at least not during their time in Italy. He asked himself again why gangsters should have wanted to carry out an act to help the Jewish people and remove from the earth a tyrant who had oppressed them ever since he had come to power in Germany. They had not killed him for money but simply out of a strange sense of idealism. There was nothing remotely idealistic about the men who lay dead by their hands.

Bellini stood rigid and with his piercing eyes tried to penetrate deep inside the souls of the two men who stood before him. Siegel and Carmona looked up to the heavens and said their final prayers. Waiting for the inevitable end, they lowered their eyes once more and stood there passively.

To their utter astonishment they saw Bellini turning around and walking away. They watched his back disappearing as he flicked his hand at the waiting police and waved them on to the other side of the port. Siegel and Carmona turned to one another and almost burst into tears.

"He knows," Carmona whispered, "and yet he let us go."

The two of them somehow found the strength of purpose and spirit to climb up the gangway that led to the *Conte di Savoia*. Before they entered the ship they turned around and took one last look. They saw Bellini in the distance and he also turned to face them and gave them one final penetrating glance before disappearing into the crowd on the dock. The two men went to their stateroom where they hugged each other. Shaking with relief, they allowed themselves to feel a rare moment of emotion.

With the realization that they were safe at last and that all their efforts had not been in vain, Siegel and Carmona headed to the ship's bar. Siegel swallowed a large shot of Bourbon while Carmona preferred a brandy. Once they had allowed the alcohol to flow through their veins each man lit a cigarette and the enormity of their achievement made them feel a sudden sense of pride.

"We did it!" Siegel said. "We did it and we lived to tell the tale! I guess we'd better see how Marianne and Celia are doing."

"They'll be all right. After all, it wasn't them who needed to worry."

"Maybe so, but I still feel like I ought to go see them."

They rejoined the women and the four of them walked along the deck as the ship slowly sailed out of port.

"Only one more stop at Naples and then we'll say goodbye to Italy," said Celia.

"It can't come soon enough for me," Siegel told her. "I just want to get home as quick as I can."

48

That night they enjoyed their first untroubled rest since they arriving in Italy. They had no fear of Bellini or gangsters and relaxed in the knowledge that they were going home at last. That expectation stayed with them throughout the voyage and even though there was still a long journey ahead hope buoyed their hearts.

They had been on the *Conte di Savoia* for four days since leaving Rome. Siegel was dancing with Marianne and Carmona sat at a table with Celia when an announcement came over the ship's radio.

The band stopped playing and the couples on the dance floor made their way back to their seats. Siegel gazed at Carmona, wondering what was about to happen next.

In the plush tones associated with the BBC an announcer read the news item.

"This is a transcript of a broadcast made earlier today on German radio by General Ludwig Beck. The general said:

MEN AND WOMEN OF GERMANY, YOU KNOW THAT OUR FÜHRER IS DEAD. AN ASSASSIN'S BULLET ROBBED HIM OF HIS LIFE AND WE WILL AVENGE HIS BRUTAL SLAYING. IN THE MEANTIME, IN THE INTERESTS OF STABILITY AND NATIONAL UNITY, THE ARMY HAS TAKEN TEMPORARY

CHARGE OF THE GOVERNMENT. WE HAVE APPOINTED THE MAYOR OF BERLIN, CARL GOERDELER, AS ACTING CHANCELLOR. OTHER GOVERNMENT POSITIONS WILL BE ANNOUNCED SHORTLY. STAY CALM AND DO NOT FEAR. CARRY ON YOUR NORMAL LIVES. WE HAVE DECIDED TO CALL FOR A WEEK OF NATIONAL MOURNING AND THE FÜHRER WILL RECEIVE A STATE FUNERAL. GERMANY WILL SURVIVE THIS TRAGIC BLOW AND WE MUST ALL COME TOGETHER AS A NATION IN THIS TIME OF SHARED GRIEF. THE FÜHRER IS DEAD BUT GERMANY LIVES FOREVER!

Total silence filled the room after the broadcast. The four of them stared intensely at each other as they absorbed the news. Taken by surprise, at first they did not react or show any emotion as they continued sipping their drinks.

Then Siegel smiled for a moment and was on the point of opening his mouth when Carmona, with an almost imperceptible shake of his head, warned him to be silent.

The atmosphere on the ship changed subtly after the broadcast. Music started up again and the dancers went back on the floor but there was a subdued feel to the proceedings.

Both men were now in a sombre mood. The enormity of what their successful mission and how the world changed because of it sapped their strength and their spirits were low.

Their mission had been successful but somehow it felt not quite real. Beck's broadcast had revealed a situation that had not been in the script for either of them. Neither man had thought beyond the mission itself. Now that the consequences seemed to be an end to the Nazi regime they found it difficult to take in the full impact of the news.

Siegel went out on deck and lit a cigarette as his eyes gazed into the blue waves of the ocean. He stared intently at the water as if searching for answers.

Carmona joined him soon after and both men looked around to make sure no one was in earshot.

"First Hitler, now this," Siegel said. "I never thought one man's death could change things so much."

He finished his cigarette and flicked it into troubled sea.

"What now? The army's in charge — does that make war more likely?"

"Who knows? Not our problem. Come on, get back inside. Marianne will be wondering where you are."

Both men tried to put the news out of their minds. Hitler was dead and changes were happening in Germany. Their job was done. All they could do was try and put it out of their minds. Their only thought now was to look forward to returning home once more.

A picture of his wife and two daughters flashed into Siegel's mind and he held on to that as a beacon of hope and normality in what had become a nightmare world. Yes, going home and seeing Esta and his girls would make it all worthwhile.

The mood among the passengers remained sombre and people were much quieter than usual. No one knew what the consequences would be and an air of anxious anticipation greeted every news bulletin.

49

Each day on board seemed to bring regular updates on the situation. It slowly became clear that the new German government was negotiating directly with the Czechs. Hopes were high for the prospects of a peaceful settlement. The chances of war over the Sudetenland looked much less likely than when Hitler was in power. Slowly the passengers began to relax and tried to enjoy their journey home.

The reaction of world leaders to Beck's broadcast was mixed. Mussolini summoned the German ambassador and demanded immediate answers.

"What has happened to the rest of the National Socialist leaders? Why has the army taken over? Do they plan any kind of military intervention in Czechoslovakia? Will they continue to assist us and Caudillo Franco against Communism in Spain? Are Italy and Germany still allies?"

The bewildered ambassador, a Nazi himself, was unable to give clear answers to these questions.

"Il Duce, I am not certain how to reply. I have received no instructions from Berlin. I imagine that Party leaders are co-operating with the new government. As to why the generals felt it necessary to — intervene I am as much in the dark as you are. I am also ignorant of any plans they may have regarding Spain or Czechoslovakia. As soon as I have further information I will of course let you know."

Mussolini realized the man was probably telling the truth and had to find other ways of discovering the information he sought. He telephoned the Italian embassy in Berlin, which appeared to know a little more about the situation.

They informed him that all the senior Nazi leaders had been arrested along with many members of the Party and leaders of the SA and SS. The situation appeared to be calm at present as the nation was still mourning for its assassinated leader. It was impossible to be sure of the future direction of the new military government but he believed that General Beck did not want to go to war over Czechoslovakia. More than that he was unable to say at present.

50

Early summer had arrived in New York and the temperature was soaring. Carmona and Siegel stood on deck together as the ship began edging its way into American waters. The skyline of New York was now visible. They knew as soon as they passed Ellis Island and the Statue of Liberty they would be home at last. A fierce sense of pride for his nation overcame Siegel.

"Just think, Luigi, my parents passed through Ellis Island to find a new life. You did the same when you left Italy to come here. You can almost taste the freedom on your breath or in the air as it whips across the city. And now we've rid the world of a tyrant who believed in oppression."

The ship docked in New York and Siegel stepped off the gangway with an immense feeling of relief. He was home at last, in America and in his city of New York. There was no sense of elation as he disembarked, rather a feeling of conquest. He was hugely proud of what he had done but now all he wanted to do now was forget everything that had happened.

It was time for him to go home. He turned to the two women, hugging and kissing them on the cheeks.

"My two beautiful girls, let me thank you for your wonderful company and hospitality. I'm going to miss you both."

After the women had left Siegel turned to Carmona. A close bond had developed between the two men and both realized their lives would never be the same. Both felt like brothers in arms.

"I still don't know the truth about you, Luigi. Maybe you are an agent for the Feds and I was just your cover. I guess I'll never know. Either way, even if you did make a sucker out of me, we killed Hitler together. Then you got us safely away and we made it back home. So whoever you are it doesn't matter now."

"You saved my life. Don't you think that means something to me?"

The two men hugged each other.

"Take care of yourself, Benny."

"You too. Maybe I'll see you around.'

He made his way out of the port. Hailing a taxi, he told the driver to take him to his hotel suite.

He took a bath and shaved off his moustache, feeling glad to see its disappearance as the last trace of stubble vanished from his now clean-shaven chin. Putting on his best summer suit, he prepared to leave the hotel. It was time for him to return home to his family.

He called another cab and on arriving home, fished the keys out of his pocked and opened the door of his apartment. The sound of his entrance roused Esta who burst into the hallway and stared at him.

"Where the hell have you been?"

Siegel felt weary and drained by the ordeal he'd been through over the last few weeks. He slumped into a chair and said nothing. She glared at him and shook him by the shoulder.

Siegel looked up at her and tried but failed to force a smile.

"I told you before, never ask me about business. It's good to be home, though."

He said goodbye to his wife and children and left to visit Lansky and Costello. Siegel swaggered along the street as he prepared to enter the restaurant. He knew that his two closest friends ate there almost every day and he looked forward to meeting them again.

As he entered the owner rushed up to greet him.

"Mr. Siegel! What a pleasure to have you back. We haven't seen you in a while."

"Well, I've been away on business. Are my friends here?"

"Yes, of course. Shall I tell them you have arrived?"

"No, let me surprise them."

With a jaunty spring in his step Siegel walked through the restaurant to the private table at the back where his two friends were having lunch.

"Hi, Meyer. Hi, Frank. How are you both?"

Costello stared in astonishment at his visitor and the food on his fork remained suspended in mid-air, its journey to his mouth arrested. Lansky almost choked on the glass of wine he was drinking and his eyes locked on to Siegel with a fierce intensity as if he doubted the evidence of his own senses. The fierce comradeship that the two men had shared since their teenage years flowed between them in a powerful surge of recognition and welcome.

"My God, you're alive, my friend."

Siegel's swagger and jauntiness left him as he sat down to join his friends. He was still shaken by events and Lansky's words were an unwelcome reminder of his ordeal.

"I don't want to talk it about. Not even with you. I've been to hell and back."

"I understand that, Benny," said Costello. "But just tell us one thing — was it you who killed four of Genovese's gang?"

"Who else would it be? Anyway, only three of them worked for Genovese. The other guy worked for Mancini and turned traitor for the reward money."

"I'll order some champagne to celebrate," said Costello, relieved that it was over and his friend had come back home safely.

Siegel's eyes then fell upon the newspaper by the side of Costello's chair. The headline read ITALY ON THE BRINK OF WAR.

Siegel's heart sank as he took in the implications of the news item. *I thought I'd changed the world for the better but now it's starting up all over again.*

CPSIA information can be obtained
at www.ICGtesting.com
Printed in the USA
LVOW03s1428191117
556905LV00003B/498/P